HEARTLESS GOON 4

Ghost

Lock Down Publications and Ca$h
Presents

HEARTLESS GOON 4
A Novel by *GHOST*

Ghost

Lock Down Publications
P.O. Box 870494
Mesquite, Tx 75187

Visit our website @
www.lockdownpublications.com

Copyright 2020 by Ghost
Heartless Goon 4

First Edition March 2020
Printed in the United States of America

Lock Down Publications
Like our page on Facebook: Lock Down Publications @
www.facebook.com/lockdownpublications.ldp
Cover design and layout by: **Dynasty Cover Me**
Book interior design by: **Shawn Walker**
Edited by: **Lashonda Johnson**

4

Stay Connected with Us!

Text **LOCKDOWN** to 22828 to stay up-to-date with new releases, sneak peaks, contests and more…

Thank you.

Submission Guideline.

Submit the first three chapters of your completed manuscript to ldpsubmissions@gmail.com, subject line: Your book's title. The manuscript must be in a .doc file and sent as an attachment. Document should be in Times New Roman, double spaced and in size 12 font. Also, provide your synopsis and full contact information. If sending multiple submissions, they must each be in a separate email.

Have a story but no way to send it electronically? You can still submit to LDP/Ca$h Presents. Send in the first three chapters, written or typed, of your completed manuscript to:

LDP: Submissions Dept
Po Box 870494
Mesquite, Tx 75187

DO NOT send original manuscript. Must be a duplicate.

Provide your synopsis and a cover letter containing your full contact information.

Thanks for considering LDP and Ca$h Presents.

Dedications:

First of all, this book is dedicated to my Baby Girl 3/10, the love of my life and purpose for everything I do. As long as I'm alive, you'll never want nor NEED for anything. We done went from flipping birds to flipping books. The best is yet to come.

To LDP'S CEO- Ca$h & COO- Shawn:

I would like to thank y'all for this opportunity. The wisdom, motivation, and encouragement that I've received from you two is greatly appreciated.

The grind is real. The loyalty in this family is real. I'm riding with LDP 'til the wheels fall off.

THE GAME IS OURS !

Ghost

Chapter 1

"Why you kill him? What if she ain't in here? What the fuck?" Shemar ignored me and jiggled the key into the lock.

He took it off and slammed it to the floor. I moved him out of the way and tried to open the door. It appeared stuck. I took one step back and kicked that bitch in as hard as I could.

As soon as it opened, I rushed inside with my heart pounding and stomach feeling like it was inside of my throat. The first thing I noticed was the heat. It was impossible to breathe. I started to panic when I saw no signs of Jahliya. All I saw was a pissy looking, dirty mattress, a thin sheet and a bowl of water that was more than half gone. I looked from left to right. The stench of sweat and piss wafted to my nose, making my stomach turn. You could most definitely tell somebody had been kept here.

"Shemar, what the fuck! Where is my sister?" I snapped. The tears of frustration finally came out of my eyes.

Shemar stepped into the doorway and rested his arm against the jamb. He lowered his head and refused to make eye contact with me. "Damn, JaMichael, I-I-I don't know."

That was it. "You don't know—you don't know?" I rushed his ass at full speed and grabbed him around the waist with the intention of slamming him as hard as I could onto his back.

Before I could get more than a few steps with him in the air, I wound up tripping over Mikey's body. I stumbled and dropped Shemar to the floor. We both landed in blood. I tried my best to get up before he could. As soon as I was up, I was rushing him again, with my fists balled.

Shemar held up his hands. "JaMichael, calm yo' ass down. I'm not the enemy. I'm wit' you lil' homie. Just—" He ducked two of my blows and got caught with the third, right in the jaw. This made him wobbly and he fell back against the wall holding his chin. "Aw, so this what we on? A'ight den lil' nigga, come on." He held his guards up on the side of his face.

I didn't care, I was hurting and felt like Shemar had taken advantage of me. I felt he knew more than he was letting on and that pissed me off more than words could express. So, I was on his ass, swinging to knock him out cold, over, and over again.

He blocked one and got hit by two, blood creased his lip and he swung with two of his own. I blocked one and got caught in the nose by his second. My shit started bleeding right away and only fueled my rage. I stumbled back a few steps.

"I don' told yo' lil' ass I'm on your side. We need to stop this stupid shit before somebody gets hurt."

I didn't give a fuck about what he was saying. I needed to feel more physical pain. I needed my mind to be taken off my sister. Her absence was driving me crazy. So, I rushed him again. This time, swinging at his head. It was like part of me wanted to see that bitch explode. I wanted to see him crumble, so I could stomp him out until my pain subsided. He had killed Mikey before we could get more information from him. *Why the fuck had he done that?* I wondered.

Shemar got hit five times, the fifth blow dropped him to his knees. He struggled to get up. When he did, he staggered around on his feet and crashed into the wall with blood dripping from the corners of his mouth and nose.

"You foul, JaMichael. What the fuck you attacking me? Nigga, I'm doing yo' father a favor. I'm doing this for, Taurus!"

I stood there with my fists balled, hurting. None of the shit he was saying registered. All I could think about was the fact my sister was supposed to be down in this basement, and she wasn't. "Fuck you, Shemar. You ain't have no right smoking that nigga until we found out where Jahliya was."

"That nigga wasn't about to tell us where your sister was, all he—" Shemar paused and looked toward the stairs. He pulled his .9 and stood beside me.

"Fuck wrong wit' chu?" I asked, taking the Glock from my waistband.

"Somebody upstairs, I heard the door open."

"Shit." I looked down at Mikey's body and the first thing I thought about was the police. I knew we were fucked. I was bussing until my clip was empty. I already had my mind made up.

There were more footsteps, then the floorboards creaked. I braced myself. "Psst. Psst." More creaking from the floorboards. "Where y'all at?" came Nikki's voice.

I breathed a sigh of relief. My heart was still pounding like crazy, though. Before I could respond I heard the muffled sound of somebody calling out to me.

"We down here, Nikki. That fool Mikey gone," Shemar hissed.

Nikki came down the stairs with two chrome Glocks in her hands. "We gotta get the fuck out of here den. We only paid the law for thirty minutes of unpatrolled time. We got five minutes left, and they gon' be through this area two squad cars deep because those fools out there showing out. So, let's go."

Shemar wiped his face, then stepped into the light. "Fuck it, let's get out of here."

"Shemar, what the fuck happened to your face?"

There were those muffled sounds again. "Shssshhh!" I ordered.

Both of them looked at me as if I were crazy. Nikki came all the way down the stairs and walked up to Shemar. She started assessing the damage to his face.

The muffled sounds came again. I tucked my gun into my waist and took off back into the room that we'd just come out of. The sounds grew louder and louder. I made haste to the closet and damn near ripped the door off its hinges before sliding it to the side.

As soon as it was opened as far as it could go, I saw her laid on her side, naked, with her mouth duct-taped. She looked as if she had lost ten pounds. Jahliya saw me and started screaming into the tape as loud as she could. I fell to my knees, took my shirt off and covered her body with it, gently pulling the tape from her mouth.

"JaMichael, get me out of here! Please get me out of here. They gon' kill me—they gon' kill both of us," she cried.

I shook my head and pulled her to my chest. "No, they ain't sis, I got you. Come on, we finna get the fuck out of here." I helped her to her feet.

She slid the shirt on and fell against me. "JaMichael, please get me out of here."

Nikki rushed into the room and placed Jahliya's arm around her neck. "Shit, JaMichael, how did you know she was in there?" Both of us took one step at a time until we got Jahliya to the top of the stairs.

"I heard her, Nikki. I swear to God I heard her."

Shemar was peeking out of the backdoor with his gun in hand. He waved us over to him. "Y'all come on, we about to make a run for it."

Jahliya seemed to get weaker, her body weight came down on me. She groaned and closed her eyes. "I feel sick, I don't know if I can run," she said hoarsely.

I wanted to unkill Mikey's ass and kill him all over again for what I could only imagine he'd done to my sister. "It's okay, Jahliya's just hold onto me."

Shemar opened the door and took a step back. It looked pitch black outside. Fireflies glowed inside the darkness. The humidity seemed to pick up steam. Somewhere off in the distance, I could hear multiple people laughing and hollering. A car sped down the street and slammed on its brakes. I didn't know what was going on in the front of the house, but in the back, me and Nikki held Jahliya up as best we could and made our way across the grass with her.

Jahliya groaned with each step she took. She had me in an almost headlock. She smelled bad like they hadn't allowed her to shower in more than a week. My heartfelt heavy and full of hatred. Even though Mikey was taken out of the equation I found myself harboring supreme need for retaliation. Somebody other than Mikey had to pay for what Jahliya had been forced to endure. Every step she took, she groaned and emitted in pain causing my heart to become more and more black.

When we made it to the alley and on the side of Shemar's van, I pulled open one of the doors in the back and helped Jahliya inside.

"There you go, sis, it's all good. We finna get you to a hospital." I kissed her forehead and closed the door. Then I jogged around to the passenger's seat of Shemar's van. He was already opening the driver's side door. "Let's roll, Shemar. Let's get t fuck out of here and get Jahliya to a hospital."

He nodded and turned over the engine. "A'ight, we gon' take her out of the city though. I got a plug over in Fort Worth. She can get some of the best healthcare in the world with no questions asked, it's all on me." He threw the van in drive.

As soon as we started to set in motion, I saw two dudes come from the back of the house that was two yards over from where we had smoked Mikey. They had choppers in their hands. One even took the time to lower himself to one knee, before he started bussing at our van.

Bloom! Bloom! Bloom! Bloom! The windows shattered as the van rocked from side to side. Jahliya screamed. I took off from the front seat and rushed to the back of the van. I unbuckled her seatbelt, towed her to the floor of the van and tossed my body on top of hers while the shots rang out.

"Shemar, get us the fuck out of here!" I hollered.

He stepped on the gas and scurted down the alley. The back windows shattered, as more rapid shots rang out in pursuit of one of us, I imagined.

"That's dem Duffle Bag niggas, JaMichael. I told you a lot of them ma'fuckas was crazy about, Mikey." He continued to storm down the alley.

When he got to the end of it and was about to enter onto the street, a black Excursion turned into the alley from the street and blocked our path. It slammed on its brakes and the doors opened. Yin appeared unmasked, along with four masked gunmen. They hopped out of her truck with assault rifles in their hands. They started airing at us right away in rapid fashions.

Bocka! Bocka! Bocka! Bocka!

The headlights of the van were shot out, along with the left front tire. The van sunk one wheel short. There were so many bullets chopping through the van, I was worried about one of them going through me and hitting Jahliya. That woulda devastated me, to say the least. Shemar threw the van in reverse and stepped on the gas. All of a sudden we were flying back at full speed with bullets coming at us. The front windshield shattered into his lap, and he kept on driving back. I don't know how he did it, but somehow, he wound up backing into an open garage. Seconds later we were pulling out of it and storming down the alley once again. He crashed into a metal shopping cart that had been left in the middle of the alley. It popped into the air and came down behind the van. Shemar kept rolling until he found the alley's other exit. Once there he turned on to the street, and the van's engine started to knock before it simply cut off and started rolling quietly.

"Oh, you gotta be fucking kidding me!" I yelled, sitting up. When I looked down the alley we'd come from, I saw the trucks storming in our direction. I knew it was over. They were armed with choppers, and all we had were handguns. I pulled Jahliya up. "Come on sis, we gotta get the fuck out of here." I didn't know where we were going or how far, but I knew we had to get a move on.

Jahliya sat up and started shaking she was sweating and shivering. "I'm sick, JaMichael, I don't feel so good."

The trucks were more than halfway through the alley. Alongside them were armed men running in our direction. Our van had rolled to a halt. "Come on y'all, hurry up, there go Nikki right there," Shemar exclaimed.

Nikki pulled up in her Chevy Caprice and blew the horn. "Y'all hurry up, here they come!"

I opened the side door of the van and eased out of it, just as more bullets begin to pop off. In a split second, they were attacking the sides of the van and rocking it from side to side. Jahliya scooted out of the van and threw up two steps into the street. She didn't have much time to finish, before the side to Nikki's car window exploded. We ducked down. Now Jahliya was coughing.

"Y'all hurry up, get her inside!" Nikki screamed.

Shemar pulled open the back door to Nikki's whip and picked Jahliya up. He forced her inside and slid in next to her. I jumped into the passenger's seat and Nikki slammed on the gas. The car's tires burnt rubber sending smoke into the air, then we shot off like a rocket.

"Man, JaMichael, what the fuck is Yin doing trying to kill you?" Nikki hollered.

"Lil' bruh don't tell me you beefing with the Chinese Triads." Shemar said, allowing Jahliya to rest her head on his thigh.

15

I felt a twinge of jealousy and anger. Jealousy because I didn't want no man comforting my sister, not after what she'd gone through and anger because of what she'd been through. "Man, it's a long story, but you remember those diamonds you paid Jefe' Pablo with?"

Shemar nodded. "Yeah, what about 'em?"

"That bitch saying they belonged to her father. That's why she at me, right now."

Nikko shook her head. "It's finna be a long rest of the year. Shemar got a lot to tell you. One thing I can say though, you are your father's son."

Shemar sighed. "Ain't that the truth."

Chapter 2

Four Months Later

"Push baby, push. Come on, daddy's right here with you," I encouraged as I wiped the sweat from Bubbie's forehead with a wet towel that had been sitting in ice water.

On the other side of the bed was Yvonne, Bubbie's mother. It had been two days since Bubbie had come to the hospital preparing to give birth, and still, Yvonne had not said more than a sentence to me.

The only two lines she'd offered was, "I can't believe you did this to my baby. You just ruined her future."

So, I knew how she felt about me and tried as best I could to avoid her at all costs.

Bubbie squeezed my hand again, I could feel the bones in it beginning to crumble. I tried as best I could to get my shit out of her grasp.

"Arrgh, don't call me your baby, right now, JaMichael! I hate your fuckin' guts! I swear to God I dooo!" She screamed, then her knees were coming back toward her shoulders.

"Kalissa, watch your mouth!" Yvonne chastised.

Kalissa was Bubbie's first name, although nobody ever called her that other than her mother. Bubbie's response was to scream some more. "I hate him, Mama! I hate him—awww!"

I was too busy feeling my hand being crushed to give a fuck what she was talking about. I closed my eyes and had to grit and bear it. "Push, Bubbie, push Mama. Come on," I encouraged, despite her confessed hatred of me.

"That's good, that's good. The baby's beginning to crown, keep on pushing. You're doing a good job, Ms. Dostier," the female doctor said, as she continued to help guide the baby out of Bubbie.

"Okay, okay!" she hollered some more. She squeezed my hand again and her eyes rolled to the back of her head at the same time mine did.

"Push! Push!" Yvonne chimed in beside the doctor.

Bubbie closed her eyes closed even tighter, the next thing I knew I was hearing the cries of our child. I breathe a sigh of relief. I expected Bubbie to release the death grip she had on my hand, but instead it was like the pressure became more intense.

The doctor pulled the baby out of her and handed it to the nurse who was leaning over Bubbie's body. She took this white thing, and wrapped it around the umbilical cord, then handed me a pair of hospital scissors. "Congratulations it's a boy. Here you go, Mr. JaMichael. Would you like to cut the umbilical cord? If so, you need to hurry, baby number two is on its way."

"*Baby number two?*" I shot daggers at Bubbie.

She kept her eyes closed, breathing heavy, sweat dripped along the side of her forehead. "Hurry up, JaMichael. I want this fuckin' thing out of me! I swear to God I ain't never having no more kids. I rather die first. Fuck this!" she screamed.

"Kalissa, language!" Yvonne chastised.

"Mama leave me alone, right now, please!"

Yvonne looked off and mumbled something under her breath. "JaMichael cut the damn cord."

I snipped it and stepped back. "There."

The doctor did her thing, the nurse stepped away with our son.

"Okay, time for baby number two. It shouldn't take long because it's already crowning. Just give it another push for me Ms. Dostier, one good one."

"I can't, I can't, my kitty hurts. I can't breathe!"

"Just push, Kalissa, you're almost done," Yvonne said picking up Bubbie's hand again.

Bubbie yanked it away. "I can't, I'm too weak!" Then she started to push anyway. She squeezed my hand with tears running down her cheeks.

All I could do was wipe her forehead with the towel I had in my right hand. "It's gon' be okay, baby. You're almost home, just push lil' mama, push for daddy."

She sat up on the pillow and pushed as hard as she could, screaming at the top of her lungs. Ten minutes later, our second son was born. We named the oldest JaMichael and the second one KaMichael. Both came out with caramel skin and deep dimples. They looked identical, with the exception of their eye coloring. JaMichael had light brown eyes while KaMichael took after Bubbie and adopted her hazel eyes. Both came out with heads full of curly hair, which was probably the reason Bubbie had complained about heartburns the further along she became during her pregnancy.

***

Jahliya didn't show up at the hospital until the next day. She was aggressive in her approach to her nephews. She had the audacity to pick Jam right up off Bubbie while he was nursing. Of, course, this didn't make him too happy. It took her ten minutes to stop him from crying. In the end, she walked around the room with both sleeping babies in her arms.

"Dang, y'all, I swear to God I love them so much already. I'm crazy about my nephews." She kissed them both and turned her back to us, while she bounced them slowly up and down in her arms. There was heavy sunlight coming in from the big bay window. It cast upon her as she did her auntie thing.

I slid on the bed beside Bubbie and kissed her forehead. "How are you feeling, baby?"

She looked run down and weak and her skin was a bit pale. "I'm tired, I feel like I just wanna sleep for the next two months. I didn't realize how much a kid could take out of a woman."

I snuggled up to her and allowed her to rest on my chest. She did so reluctantly. "Thank you, boo."

She picked her head up and looked up at me as if I had lost my mind. "Why are you thanking me?"

I nodded my head over at a singing Jahliya. She bounced the babies up and down and began to dance just slightly with them.

"For those beautiful babies. You are amazing and I just wanted to let you know that." I kissed her forehead again.

She smiled shortly, then pushed me away. "Get off me, JaMichael. I'm still mad at you." She mugged me and laid her head back on her pillow.

"Mad at me for what?" I played stupid.

"You know why, but I ain't finna get into all that, right now. I don't have the patience nor energy to do so. What are you going to do about, Tamia?" she asked, picking a piece of lint off my Polo t-shirt.

"What do you mean?"

"JaMichael, she's about to have your baby, too. How are you about to divide your time and energy between two houses? I'm not about to have me and my sons placed on the back burner for nobody. So, what are you going to do?" she asked, yawning.

"I'ma do what I'm supposed to do. I'ma take care of my bidness with her and do what I'm supposed to do with you as well. It's as simple as that." I rubbed the side of her face.

She smacked my hand away, sat up and grabbed me by the shirt. "Look, nigga, all that bouncing around you were doing before I had these kids was fuck shit but me being dumb, I allowed you to do whatever you wanted. Well as of today, July the twenty-ninth, it's a new day. You're either finna be faithful and stand up, or you can go on about your business. Which is it going to be?"

Jahliya walked closer to the bed. "He finna be faithful, or I'm finna kick his ass. You just had two of his kids, girl and you just turned eighteen a few months ago. He owes you more than his faithfulness. Hell, he owes you two lives. Since he can't give you two lives like you gave him, he finna give you the only one he has. It's as simple as that." She kissed first JaMichael, then KaMichael.

Bubbie smiled. "Thank you, sis. I'm so glad you are home."

"I got chu, JaMichael know not to mess with me. Ain't that right, lil' bruh?"

I laughed. "Yeah, that's right." were the words that came out of my mouth, but in my brain was a different story.

I already felt pussy deprived because Bubbie hadn't given me none in almost two months. Tamia was acting funny, too, but that was only because of her jealousy of Bubbie. I didn't know what life was going to be like once Tamia had my seed, but so far, I found myself miserable. Even with all the money that I was beginning to rake in working under Jefe' Pablo and Shemar.

"Well, that still ain't giving me a clear answer. Who are you about to be with? Is it going to be me or her?"

"Bubbie we ain't finna get into all that, right now. I wanna enjoy the fact that I am a father, and that you have just given me two healthy twin boys, that look like a perfect blend of me and you."

"JaMichael, I ain't trying to hear that shit. You need to answer me. All you're doing is beating around the bush."

Jahliya eased the twins into their cribs on each side of Bubbie's bed. She looked over at me and our eyes locked. "Well, gon' 'head and answer her lil' brother. She deserves to know what you finna do. Just keep that shit real." She placed her hand to her lips and paused. "Dang I gotta remember, I can't be cursing around these Angels like that." She popped herself in the mouth.

"I know, it's gon' take some getting used to," Bubbie said, before turning her head sideways and bugging her eyes at me? "Well?"

My phone vibrated with a text from Shemar.

Shemar: Hey JaMichael, you got a few minutes to video chat?

Me: Give me a half-hour. I have some family issues to tend to.

"Look, I don't feel like going back and forth, right now. I don't know how I'm gon' feel about Tamia after she has my child. I don't want to look too far into things. I got way too much stuff on my plate to be thinking about relationships, and all of that. When the bottom line is, I'ma handle my bidness as a man no matter what."

"Well, you ain't gotta put me and my kids on your to-do list. I will figure things out, even if I gotta be on my own. Trust and believe that." She pulled her sheets up over her breasts and sighed. I could tell she was irritated, and I didn't give a fuck. "I already know you finna be on some bullshit, Ja-Michael. When will you grow up?"

Now I was super annoyed because it felt like she was trying to pick wit' me for whatever reason. "Man shut the fuck up, I don't wanna hear that shit already. Give me some time to get acquainted wit' my kids before you try to shut them off, wit' yo' selfish ass."

Bubbie looked shocked. "*Selfish*! I'm selfish? Are you fuckin kidding me, right now? After I just laid on my back and pushed out your two big-headed ass kids? Carried them for over nine months while you ran around fuckin' every bitch your dick could fit into, including Danyelle, your fuckin' cousin! Don't you dare tell me I'm selfish. Negro if anybody is selfish it's yo' black ass," she snapped, then rose up just enough for the sheet to fall off her to her waist.

I frowned and felt myself about to lose it. "Bitch, I'm so sick of—"

"Whoa, whoa, whoa," Jahliya said rushing over blocking my path before I could make it to Bubbie's bed. She musta seen the look of '*I don't give a fuck*', written all over my face. She took a hold of me and ushered me in the other direction. "Come with me this way, JaMichael."

***

We wound up on the eight floor Men's bathroom with the door locked. She stood in front of me with her piercing brown eyes and rested both of her little hands on my chest. "You okay?"

I shook my head. "N'all, that girl driving me crazy already. I don't know what the fuck to do."

Jahliya smiled and looked off, then back into my eyes again. "Now that she got your kids, JaMichael, you can't be calling that girl no bitch. She officially has become a Queen your Queen to be exact. Them lil' boys hear you calling their mother out of her name, either one or two things are going to happen. They are either going to think it's sweet to call the women of their lives the same thing, and they'll have very little respect for women in general. Or, they will grow up to hate and resent you. Either way, neither alternative is okay. So, you need to nip the way you talk to their mother in the bud right away. Do you hear me?"

I nodded. "Yeah."

"A'ight, now I know you feel pressured to make a decision and that's irritating, but she got a right to know what's to be expected once this other girl has your baby. You gotta see things through her eyes, not just your own. It's only fair." She stroked the side of my face and kissed my lips, with her eyes closed, then she opened them and was looking directly into mine. "Now look, I love you, JaMichael, and I got your back. You ain't in this shit alone, trust me."

I did and her affection, words of discipline and encouragement were enough to calm me down for a little while. I didn't know what lied ahead, but at least for that moment I was able to relish in the fact that Jahliya was home, and she had my back, especially since I was going to need it.

Chapter 3

Shemar handed me a double cup of Purple Danger and smiled. "Nigga this shit here is the hottest Lean going around Houston, it's my own personal mix. This shit about to have yo' ass lit like dynamite," he jacked before picking up a thick stack of hundred-dollar bills and placing them into the money counter. The machine took effect right away.

I sipped from the cup, I could smell the medicine. It was thick as syrup and sweet as melted candy. Five minutes after sipping, back to back, the double cup was a quarter of the way down, and I was having a hard time keeping my eyes open. I felt breezy, I felt like a boss and pain-free. The *Lil' Baby* album beating through the speakers seemed to make a million percent more sense to me. I didn't even know if a million percent was possible, but it's what I felt like.

I scooted to the front of the black leather couch and picked up a stack of money, clicked on my money machine, and set the stack of cash into the feeder. It made a loud noise, before inhaling the bills, and counting them swiftly. My eyelids were heavy. They felt like somebody was trying to pull them down to my chin. I wanted to drop my head in my lap, but I knew I had to stay awake and alert. My forehead got as close as my lap before I snapped awake.

Shemar's eyelids were slit. "That's that shit, right there, ain't it, nephew?"

I nodded and wiped the drool from my mouth. "Hell yeah, this shit got me leaning like a ma'fucka that need a cane." I stuffed the first twenty thousand into the duffel bag, after putting a rubber band around it. Jefe' Pablo was real particular. He wanted twenty thousand-dollar knots, no less. He was the leader of the Cartel that had given me the green light to take Mikey out, head of the Duffel Bag Cartel, so I could get

Jahliya back from captivity. Now that I had her back, he figured he had held up his end of things and expected me to do the same. My end of things was to shut Tennessee completely down and flood it with Jefe' Pablo's tar. He expected no less than fifteen million in sales a month, my life and the lives of those I loved, including Shemar and his family depended on that quota being filled. When I had first heard that number, I thought he was out of his mind. I didn't even think it was feasible to come up with that much paper, but Shemar quickly showed me how.

He helped to build a team of hustlers around me all over the state, it was because of him that I was meeting Jefe' Pablo's expectations and even exceeding them. After fifteen million I was free to hustle his product that I'd copped on the side, and what I made from it was strictly mine. So far, I was averaging about a hundred and fifty gees a month, which was good math, but I knew it could be better. I wanted to live in a mansion like Shemar and Nikki. Both worked under Jefe' Pablo and both seemed to have the Game figured out.

Shemar filled one of his duffel bags and zipped it up. He pulled another empty one closer to him and started doing the same thing. "You see, JaMichael, once we get dude's shit out of the way every month, we're free to do our own thing. That's why the first fifteen million I make every month I send that shit off right away. I been averaging about two and a half weeks. That gives me a week and a half to go hard for myself. After I make his cash it's always plenty Tar baby left over."

Tar baby was what we called Mexican heroin. The reason we called it Tar Baby was because it came black as tar, and sticky as tar before it was ironed out. Getting it straight from Jefe' Pablo, the dope was often about ninety-five percent. Most Tar that was sold on the streets wasn't more than fifty percent pure. So, at ninety-five percent it gave us a lot of room to work with. We could step on our work three times and it would still be more potent than the rival's best work. Being connected to the Cartel had its plusses, that was for sure.

"I'm adopting that same philosophy. But I'm only leaving myself with about four days to hustle for me and my causes after I get him right. I'm still getting the hang of this shit, that's all." I was already at two hundred thousand in my duffel bag. I damn near fell asleep as I was placing a new knotted bundle inside the bag. The Lean had me twisted.

Shemar ran his hand over his face and tried his best to open his eyes all the way. "We finna do the damn thang tonight, JaMichael. I'm finally cutting the velvet rope on my new strip club and casino. It's the first one in Texas. This bitch finna be turnt. One day I'ma have a whole Chain of these ma'fuckas." He closed his eyes and started snoring while slowly leaning to his right. Before his head could hit the arm of the couch, he opened them and went right back to doing what he was doing as if nothing happened.

I started cracking up with my eyes closed. I was just as fucked up. I bucked my eyes and smacked my lips. My mouth was drier than the desert. Gucci everythang."

"What?" Shemar asked, closing his eyes again. His head fell forward on his neck. He started to snore for a full minute.

That made me sleepy, so I joined him, but only for about thirty seconds. I placed another bundle on the money counter. When I started it up Shemar's eyes popped wide open. He wiped his mouth. "Gucci everythang what that means? That a Memphis term or somethin'?"

"Nall nigga, I'm telling you that's what I'm rocking. Gucci from head to toe."

Shemar smiled. "Bet those. Speaking of that, yo' birthday next month, but I got something for you this month to celebrate your fatherhood and your birthday." He tried to stand up and wound up sitting back down. He broke into short laughter and I joined him.

"Damn, nigga, I thought you said you was the chef of this Lean we double cupping?" I said, laughing at his ass.

He took a second to gather himself. He rubbed his eyes with his fists and yawned. "I am, but I think I put my foot in this shit too much. It done rocked my ass."

I added ten thousand dollars to my duffel bag that Jefe' Pablo's treasurers were set to pick up at midnight. "Yeah, well, I already know them bitches finna be popping, especially tonight. Make sure you keep ya nephew with a few ducked off to the side? Hit a nigga wit' a six or something." I smiled, serious as hell though.

"I got you, I'ma slap a twelve to the side and you can fuck wit' it as you see fit." He gathered himself again and used the couch to stand up by the use of the arm. Once up, he took a second to stretch his arms over his head, yawned and shook his head. Then he stepped to the back of the den, pulled the closet door to the side, reached inside and came out with a trunk. He kneeled, opened the Louis Vuitton trunk and tossed me two bulletproof Kevlar vests. They were heavy and landed on my lap like a ton of bricks.

I stood up and pulled my shirt over my head. I started sliding my arms into the holes of one of the vests right away. I already knew what they were. "It's about time, now we talking."

Shemar laughed. "Nephew you can try that on without a shirt, but from here on out you gon' need to rock at least a beater over your bare skin before you put that on. Just in case you do gotta feel them slugs that cloth a prevent that shit from burning you too bad. But either way this the best defense against them slugs. This is Kevlar's latest edition."

I had that bitch on and hooked around me. It felt like I had on a heavy, but thin layer of football pads. I paced back and forth with it. "Yeah, I can do this, but it's gon' take some getting used to."

Shemar nodded. "Now that you fuckin' with the Cartel, and you getting your money all the way up its gon' be plenty cats trying to take you out of the game. We gon' also get you a die-hard, head bussing, security team, that's gon be about that life for you. You represent a whole lot of money, Ja-Michael, and lives. If anything happens to you, not only will it kill your father, but Jefe' Pablo gon' send them hittas to whack everything I'm affiliated with."

"Including me," Nikki said, stepping her thick ass into the room. She was rocking a Chanel dress that was so tight I could see her hard nipples poking through the material. "Hey, y'all."

I looked her up and down and felt my piece twitching. Nikki was caramel-skinned, with brown eyes and Asian like eyes. She was slim up top, but she had some nice D cup titties, with big nipples. I knew that from experience. Her waist was also slim, but her ass, and thighs were fat. They went perfectly with her five-feet-six, frame.

"What's good, Nikki?"

She came over and slid her arms around my body. "Ain't nothing to it nephew." She pissed my cheek. "Uh Shemar, did you forget that you're supposed to be meeting Nicole at the airport in twenty minutes?"

"Aw shit!" Shemar jumped up and headed upstairs. "Lil' bruh, I'ma fuck wit' you when I get back. Damn, Nikki, how you let me forget?"

She waved him off. "That girl eighteen now, she finna give you all that you can handle, too. Her and her mama."

29

"Damn, I did say Syndie could come. What the fuck was I thinking? I'll see y'all in about an hour. JaMichael, you be ready to roll out." He rushed up the stairs.

"I will be." I gave it a full minute before I stepped to Nikki. I grabbed her by her little waist and pulled her to me. "Damn, you smell good."

She smiled and looked into my eyes. "Oh, is that right?"

"Hell, yeah, that's right." My hands were all over her ass. The material was so flimsy that when I cuffed it, I could feel her heat. It felt so good. My weakness had always been older women.

She moaned when my hand slipped in between her legs and up her gap. She had on a pair of thongs that were lost deep in her crack. Her perfume was intoxicating. It was like she was placing me under her spell, just the scent of her. She looked into my eyes, and slid her hand in between us, cuffing my piece. She squeezed it and kissed my neck. "Damn, lil' daddy, I knew you was gon' be back for some of this vet shit. What dem lil' young hoes ain't enough for you?"

In response, I picked her up and fell against the wall with her. The Lean had me a little woozy, I had to gain my consciousness right away or we would of fall to the ground. Nikki wrapped her thighs around me right away. She sucked my lips and trailed her tongue all over them.

"Hurry up and fuck this pussy lil' daddy."

Fuck it. I fell to the floor with her and wound up right between her thighs, pushed that dress up, and ripped her thongs clean off her. She moaned and yelped at the same time. Then there was her trimmed pussy, all fat, and engorged. The lips looked as if they were breathing. I rubbed them for a second and planted kisses over the top where her clit poked out at me like an erect nipple. I sucked hard on it, she arched her back and opened her thighs wider.

"Shit JaMichael, get yo ass up here. I just need a quickie we can do all that extra shit later."

I followed her wishes and climbed up her body. She took a hold of my pipe and forced it into her sex lips. I sank deep, punching into her warmth. Before I was six inches inside my hips started going. Both of her ankles were placed on my shoulders, then I was plunging at full speed as hard as I could, while her titties worked themselves out of her dress top. Both brown nipples looked like erasers.

"Uh, uh, uh. Talk that nephew shit now," I said hitting that pussy hard.

"Uh, uh-uh, shut up! Aaahhh, JaMichael, baby, shit this young dick." She screamed and locked me between her thighs. She dug her nails into my sides and came hard. Her cat started quivering all around me. It felt like she got hotter and hotter.

I pushed her back and really started hitting that shit, sucking loudly on her neck. "This my pussy, Nikki. This my shit." I fucked her harder, and faster. "I love, uh-uh-uh, this vet shit." I bit into her neck and came, jerking inside of her.

She leaned all the way back and groaned, before cumming again. She leaned all the way forward and wrapped her arms around my neck with me still deep inside of her. Her tongue lashed out and licked my lips. Her breathing remained heavy. She wiped the sweat from my forehead with her thumbs. "Ja-Michael, I hope you been doing right by Jefe' Pablo. I know the new position gon' take some getting used too. Whatever you do, please don't get comfortable. You gotta remember that all of our lives are at stake with each move you make." She kissed along my neck and stood up, leaving my pipe sticking straight up, and shiny with her juices. She looked down at him and smiled.

I stood upright along with her. "Nikki why y'all always finding a way to remind me of how crazy this, Jefe' Pablo is?

All y'all had to do was say it one time, I get it." I followed her into the bathroom and proceeded to run the shower.

She was obviously thinking the same thing because she wound up stripping naked and dropping her clothes before I even had the chance too. I watched the beams of water ricochet off her sexy body, it only deepened my obsession with older women. Nikki was so fine to me.

"Baby, I personally just want to make sure you're on your game. That's all there is to it. You have all the tools inside of you to be great in this game, but I don't feel like you'll reach your full potential if me and Shemar don't stay on yo' ass, it's as simple as that." She soaped up the towel and took a hold of my dick, before washing it up. "I still can't believe you got all of this meat. Damn, I wish I was fifteen years younger. I'd lock yo ass down. You better stay away from Nicole when she gets here, too. Shemar will have a fit about that lil' girl." She stroked me and made it lay right up against her stomach, before squeezing it again and running her small hand up and down it.

"Who is, Nicole?"

"Shemar's daughter, his pride and joy! Stay away from her, or it's gon' ruin you and his relationship."

I nodded and grabbed her by the ass cheeks. "Cool, Nikki, now bring yo ass here, let me hit this vet pussy again."

Chapter 4

Later that night, Shemar took me to his underground garage that was equipped with some of the hottest foreign cars I had ever seen in my life. My eyes roamed around the underground car heaven until he stopped and pulled a tarp off a brand-new, fire red Porsche, with Lamborghini doors. It set on red and black rims and had tints.

"Before I was interrupted by my obligations earlier, I wanted to bring you downstairs and give you your early birthday present." He held the keys out to me. "Here, this is for you, enjoy."

I know he was talking about the whip, but I couldn't take my eyes off the fine ass young woman that was under his arm. She was five-feet-five inches tall, light-skinned, with green eyes, and long curly hair that stopped somewhere in the middle of her back, and she wore Chanel glasses. I didn't know if they were for fashion or if they were for real usage, either way, they made her look good as hell to me. Shemar walked with her possessively under his right arm. He held her so close, I couldn't even see if she had ass or not. Her chest was only slightly poked out, but from as far as I could see it went with her frame.

"So, what do you think?" he asked dropping the keys into my hands.

Me and Nicole's locked eyes. She blushed and looked down at the ground. I could tell she was sheltered. That shit turned me on.

Shemar saw how I was peeping her and looked down at his daughter. "Say, Nicole, why don't you go upstairs with your mother, baby? Let me holla at my nephew, gon now." He patted her on the butt.

"Okay." She kept her head down and hurried in the direction of the elevator that would take her to the first-floor portion of the house.

As soon as she walked off, I looked down at that ass. I couldn't believe my eyes. Her backside was poked out like a six-month pregnant belly inside her Prada skirt dress. She had a sexy bow-legged walk, and all I knew was my heart started pounding in my chest. Before the elevator doors closed, we locked eyes again, then she looked down and off to her left.

Shemar waited until the elevator door closed, before he dropped his head and shook it from left to right, sighing. "Ja-Michael, JaMichael, JaMichael, let's nip this shit in the bud, right now. You can't fuck with my daughter under no circumstances."

"What?" I asked, playing the fool.

"Boy, you heard me. You don't think I saw the way you was looking at her? That's a no-no, right there, nephew." He took a sip from his double cup of Purple Danger.

"Shemar you tripping, I was just admiring her beauty. I would never come at her in no way knowing how you feel about her. It's all good." I was already imagining what Nicole would look like sprawled out naked in a Penthouse Suite. I couldn't wait to get my hands on her, my tongue too.

"Well, good, because I know we always telling you about how dangerous, Jefe' Pablo is. Well, when it comes to my daughter, that nigga ain't got shit on me. While she's down here visiting from Brooklyn, I need you to be my second pair of eyes. We're all family and I don't trust nobody with my daughter, nephew, but I trust you. You feel me? Just keep that shit one hunnit wit' me, Playboy." He shook my hand and gave me a half hug.

I patted his back once and broke our embrace. "I got you, believe that. Now let me check Shawty out, right here," I said stepping past him, over to the red Porsche. While I listened to him explain all the features the Porsche had, all I kept thinking about was Nicole, and how that ass jiggled all the way to the elevator.

***

At midnight we were up in Shemar's new Gentlemen's club, and Casino. I was up four thousand at the craps table and shaking the dice in my hand when Nicole came and eased her way into the slight crowd of spectators that were around the table. I smiled at her and she smiled back. I blew into my fist and rolled the dice. They bounced off the lip of the table and rolled to eleven.

"Eleven, winner." The person in charge of the table announced.

I grabbed two more hundred and added it to my pile of chips. "This shit light work, here." I added up a thousand-dollars, worth of chips then tossed them in front of the table manager.

"Bet a thousand, shoot a thousand, all bets locked in. The men and women placed their side bets all around the table.

I shook the dice and rolled them, bitches looking Nicole in the eyes. She sucked on her bottom lip and looked at the table. The dice rolled to a five and a four. She looked up at me.

"Nine, nine is the point, place your bets," the table manager encouraged.

I added another thousand to my pile of chips. I was on some flexing shit. Nicole was bad as a muthafucka, I had to play the part of a boss nigga, just in case that shit turned her on or something. I really wasn't trying to lose a penny, but if it took me losing a penny to pick up a dime, I was all for it.

"Alright, bets are locked in, shooter shoot."

I shook the bitches in my fist again and rolled them across the table. They came up on a two and a three. Some of the betters started picking up their chips, while others encouraged me to roll again. My focus was strictly on her. I shook the dice in my hand and blew into my fist, before rolling them again. This time I rolled them hard enough to bounce off the lip all the way at the end of the table. The dice hit the lip and bounced up, before coming down on a six, and a three. I smiled.

"Point made." The table manager scooted my chips over to me.

I rushed and stacked them into the tray, before coming and standing beside Nicole. She smelled like expensive cherries or something. From up close, I could see she wore a thin coat of makeup, and she did the best she could to cover up two pimples that were along her chin. Though they were there they did very little to take away from her beauty.

"What's good, Shawty, I never got a chance to properly introduce myself. My name is—"

"JaMichael, I know who you are. You're from Memphis, you got two kids and one on the way that should be here any day now. Your children are by two different women, or should I say girls my age, and you technically ain't with either one of them. You work under my father by way of, Mr. Jefe' Pablo. You're a very dangerous man and stay in dangerous positions. I've been advised for my own safety to stay away from you. Nothing good can come from establishing a relationship with you is what I am being told." She stepped down from the table and proceeded to walk through the casino portion of Shemar's establishment.

Right away my eyes went to that fat ass booty. She was rocking this *Givenchy* dress that clung to her every curve. I had to have this bitch, I didn't give a fuck what Shemar or she was talking about.

I caught up to her still carrying my chips. "So, I'm saying, you finna shoot me down before I even have the chance to fill you in on my side of things? What type of shit is that?"

She stopped and turned to look at me. "JaMichael, I just turned eighteen. I am booked on the next upcoming season of *Black Lightning*. Recently signed a one-year contract with Cover girl cosmetics, and this fall I will be going to Harvard to obtain my law degree. What do we possibly have in common?"

I couldn't do nothing but look in her green eyes. "Damn, you so fine." I felt mesmerized.

"Exactly." She started walking again. I started following on side of her. "If I know my father, he told you to stay away from me. If I were you, I would listen. You ain't got no wins over here. You're not my type. You have no future that I can bet on." As she got closer to the front of the Casino, two of Shemar's bodyguards came out of seemingly nowhere and stepped on each side of her protectively. "Bye, JaMichael, go turn those chips in or something and have a good night."

I stood there stuck, watching her juicy booty sway from left to right. It looked so, so good. "Damn, that bitch bad," I said out loud.

Nikki came and slid her arm around my neck. "What's good, nephew, you alright?"

I nodded my head with everything Nicole had just said to me still deep in my mind. I felt like a straight loser. "Yeah, I'm good."

"I see you been hitting our pockets," she said, eyeing the chips that I won playing craps.

"Yeah, a lil' bit."

She frowned and looked me over closer. "You sure you're alright?"

"Yeah, I just got some shit on my mind, I'm good though."

"A'ight cool, come on, let me introduce you to some of the dancers that's about to help me and Shemar turn this bitch into a million-plus dollar a year club." She took hold of my hand and pulled me to the other side of the club.

***

I sat beside Nikki in the private room while two thick ass strippers, one dark-skinned with purple hair, and one white girl with snow-white hair rubbed all over her. They licked along her neck and both of their hands disappeared up her skirt. In seconds she was moaning, with her head tilted all the way back. The white girl got on her knees and pulled Nikki's skirt all the way back. She spread her thighs apart and stuck her face into her gap, then she was slurping while Nikki placed her heels on the couch pillows.

The dark-skinned stripper walked over to me and sat on my lap. She smelled like cinnamon and wore a red two-piece. Her titties were already out, and the bottom portion of the two-piece was in her ass.

"So, you're this JaMichael that all of us girls keep on hearing about?" She licked my ear.

I nodded. "Yeah, that's me. What all did you hear, Shawty?"

She sucked my neck and trailed her hand down to my lap. Once there she unzipped my Gucci jeans and slipped her hand inside the opening. She pulled my dick out and proceeded to stroke him at a medium speed. My eyes were across the way. The white girl had Nikki's thighs wide open and fingering her at full speed while she sucked on her clit. Nikki was moaning loud and forcing the girl's face into her crotch even more. The dark-skinned stripper dropped to her knees and sniffed my head.

"Bitch tell me what you heard?"

She groaned. "Damn, daddy, you gon get me wet talking to me like that."

I grabbed her by her hair and guided her to my piece. She sucked him into her mouth right away. As soon as her heat enveloped me, I saw Nicole's ass and imagined what it would feel like to fuck her thick ass from the back. I leaned back on the couch and guided her head up and down while she did her thing. "Mmm, bitch what you hear?"

She popped me out and licked around the head. "I heard you're the new king of Memphis." She sucked me all the way down and came up again, pulling me out. "They say you're set to take over Tennessee. That you personally dismantled them Duffel Bag Cartel niggas for what they did to your sister. And that you're Taurus's son." She sucked me back in and really started going crazy.

I reached across her back and gripped that ass. That didn't distract her from doing her thing in the least bit. She simply moaned around me and continued to give me her best head game.

Nikki kneeled on the sofa and held the back of it while the white stripper went to town on her. She balled her hands into fists and proceeded to beat on the back of the couch with her head tilted toward the ceiling.

Her eyes were closed tightly. "Fuck, do me, baby. Shit!"

The snow bunny opened her cheeks further, all I could see was her tongue traveling in figure eights around Nikki's clit from the back. Then she was sucking and pulling in it. This sent Nikki into a screaming rage. She slid two fingers into herself and came hard, falling against the back of the couch. The white girl kept on eating as if she were trying to drive Nikki out of her mind.

As soon as Nikki screamed I couldn't help but to cum. My toes curled up in my Balenciaga's. I pushed the dark-skinned stripper away, and came all over her face, before sliding it back into her mouth imagining that it was Nicole.

"Yeah, bitch, take that. Everything you heard about me is one hunnit, the streets are mine."

***

About two-thirty that night, Shemar, called me into his office that was located at the top of the club. When I came in Phoenix was already seated in the leather seat across from Shemar's desk. He saw me and stood up holding his hand out so I could shake it.

Instead of shaking it, I mugged his ass and looked over at Shemar. "Fuck is this nigga doing in here?" Shemar motioned for me to take a seat, I refused. "You can tell me what's good. I don't need to sit down."

Shemar nodded at Phoenix and he sat. Then he turned to me. "Look, JaMichael, I already know you're not about to like what I'm about to say but you have to hear me out with open ears, and an open mind. Do you understand me?"

"I'm listening."

Phoenix looked off. "It's finna be a war, I already see this shit."

"Fuck you say?" I asked, stepping past Shemar's desk over to him.

Phoenix jumped up and slid his hand under his shirt. He pulled out a .40 Glock and cocked it. "Bitch ass nigga, ain't nobody got time for this. I'd rather splatter yo' ass and get it over with."

"What?" I upped both .9s and cocked them.

Chapter 5

Shemar jumped up and held out his hands. "Whoa, whoa, whoa, now you lil' niggas gotta chill. This shit ain't finna go down like that. Phoenix, sit yo ass down. JaMichael, you take a seat behind my desk. We finna figure this shit out, right now."

"Man, fuck that! Me and this nigga got personal bidness that shit you talking can wait," I snapped.

"Daddy, I—" Nicole started, sticking her head into the door. Then she looked from me to Phoenix and saw that we both had heaters in our hands. "Aaahhh, damn."

Shemar hurried to the door and closed it. "Baby, I'll talk to you later. Go downstairs and find Nikki, tell her to get her ass up here."

"Okay, Daddy!" Nicole hollered.

I never took my eyes off Phoenix. I wanted to pop his ass. I knew how Shemar got down. If I popped Phoenix and left his noodles all over his desk, he couldn't do shit but help me clean up the mess. I had a serious hatred for him, and anybody associated with the Duffle Bag Cartel. That was the group of niggas that were once led by Mikey, the fuck nigga that had kidnapped my sister Jahliya and demanded a ransom in order for me to receive her back safe and sound. Deep in my heart, I knew Phoenix had something to do with everything, but I couldn't quite figure out just how involved he really was.

"Both of you lil' niggas, sit the fuck down, right now!" Shemar snapped.

Phoenix kept mugging me for a second. Then he trailed his eyes over to Shemar and took a seat on the couch. He slipped his gun back under his shirt and fixed his clothes once again. He was rocking so much gold jewelry it looked ridiculous.

"JaMichael?"

"I heard you." I took a seat behind the desk, set both of my guns on Shemar's desk, and purposely angled them toward Phoenix. I still hadn't made up my mind on whether I was going to smoke his ass or not.

Shemar ran his hands over his deep waves and looked from me to Phoenix. "Say Mane, both of you lil' niggas about to be in for a rude awakening. As of tomorrow, you two muthafuckas are being assigned by Jefe' Pablo himself to work beside one another. Y'all are to split Tennessee down the middle, but you both are equally responsible for the entire state, and the sales that go on when it comes to Jefe' Pablo's Tar Baby, and Powder."

"*What?*" I said, jumping up. "I don't need no help from this snake ass nigga. I got Tennessee under control. This fuck nigga ain't even from the homeland. Why don't they assign him to Arizona or some shit?"

Phoenix stood up. "Nigga, please me a Mikey had that bitch juking before your lil' privileged ass hopped off the porch. Nigga, I swear you wouldn't be shit if yo' Pops wasn't who he is. You riding the fuck out of Taurus's legacy, straight up."

"Bitch nigga, well, how about I become a legend by blowing the front of yo' face-off den? What you think about that?" I said getting heated.

"Enough!" Shemar slapped his hands together. "Both of you muthafuckas nagging like bitches. Shut the fuck up, or we can light this muthafucka up like a Christmas Tree." He came around the desk, bumped me out of the way, pulled open the bottom drawer and came up with a Mach-90. He grabbed the hundred and fifty round clip from the top drawer. The clip hung from the handle like a Pez dispenser.

"Man, you already know I ain't on that shit, Shemar. I know how Jefe' Pablo gets down, I ain't trying to fuck wit' that crazy-ass Mexican, or them Sinaloa muthafuckas, but I ain't got no fuckin' choice. Y'all need to teach this goofy ass nigga that."

Nikki tapped on the door and opened it. She stepped into the room, closing the door behind her. The first person she laid her eyes on was me. Then she looked down at the guns on the desk. "What the fuck going on up in here?"

Shemar shook his head. "These dumb ass niggas ready to kill each other."

"Did you tell them that they are cousins?"

"That nigga ain't got my blood running through him," I snapped.

Nikki nodded her head. "Yes, he do, that's Taurus's nephew. His father is your father's blood brother."

Phoenix lowered his head. "That shit don't mean nothing."

"Wait, so this shit true?" I asked him.

He ignored me. "Anyway, how dis shit finna work? What we split Tennessee down the middle or somethin'?"

"I wish it was that simple, but n'all, it don't work like that. Unfortunately, Jefe' Pablo found out you two are related, and that both of you descend from Taurus. He thinks two heads are better than one, that he'll make more money if both of you are working together. Phoenix since you were second in command of the Duffel Bag Cartel, he wants you to step into the leadership role, and take over the day to day operations. Mikey grossed him close to fifty million a month. He's confident you can do the same. JaMichael, you have ties directly to Taurus. He wants you to use them to extend the business Eastern of Tennessee, but that's not all—" Shemar sat on the desk and looked over to Nikki.

Nikki took a deep breath and slowly exhaled. "There is a war going on between the Sinaloa Cartel and Jefe' Pablo's. The territory that both are looking at to keep a stronghold on is Phoenix. Phoenix is the gateway to the drug importing from Mexico into the United States. Whichever Cartel controls Phoenix, they control the entire country."

Shemar stood back up. "Jefe' Pablo wants us to enter into that war. Anybody that's associated with the Sinaloa Cartel we are to crush them. He will give me a list of enemies to attack, and before that month is out that list is to be fulfilled. No excuses are permitted."

"But on the flip side, the Sinaloa Cartel will be issuing out the same list to their employees, or what have you," Nikki chimed in.

"Which means we are all targets to be annihilated. Anybody that is in direct dealings with Jefe' Pablo is seen as an enemy of the Sinaloa. Which means we are all in jeopardy and those we love," Shemar added.

"Yeah, so we ain't got time to be beefing with each other or to be squashing feuds between two grown-ass men. We need to work together and stay alive," Nikki said.

All this shit was blowing my mind. "You mean to tell me that not only are all of us slaves and gotta push Jefe' Pablo's dope all over these Southern states for the rest of our lives but on top of that, now we gotta be soldiers in his army?" I asked, disbelieving the position I found myself in.

Shemar nodded. "It's the price of balling, JaMichael. Ma'fuckas be thinking being rich in the game is all happiness and bottle popping, that's a lie, a straight-up fairy tale. I ain't never met a happy kingpin. All of us be so worried about this and that, that we find ourselves going crazy. It's very little room for happiness and celebration. That's just the way the game is designed."

Phoenix shook his head. "I already know all this shit. The fact that he didn't makes me very nervous. Ain't no room for error here. This nigga ain't street certified, I am. I got Memphis, muthafuckas know Phoenix. Muthafuckas ride for Phoenix." He mugged me. "All niggas know when it comes to him, is Taurus. What the fuck is my uncle's legacy gon' do for me? Don't nobody give a fuck about that old shit. I represent the new South. Taurus is ancient news."

I laughed. "Shut the fuck up, that nigga Mikey had yo ass shook and in hiding. You wasn't on shit. You wanna know where Mikey at, right now?" I asked lowering my eyes. "That nigga lifeless, resting in hell, you lucky, you ain't his roommate. But on my seeds bitch nigga, I don't give a fuck what you is to me. If Jahliya ever tells me you hurt her in any way, fuck Jefe' Pablo, fuck Shemar, fuck Nikki, fuck this understanding. I'm smoking yo' pussy ass and I'ma piss on yo grave."

Phoenix nodded. "Yeah, that I would love to see." He laughed and stood up. "Shemar, check yo' boy and get his mind right before I buss his brains. I wear that killa shit on my heart, not my necklace. Y'all get in touch wit' me when this contract goes into effect. For now, I gotta bounce from this room before I do somethin' that would affect all our lives."

He shook Shemar's hand and went to give Nikki a kiss on the cheek, but she moved her head away. "Don't say stupid shit like that, Phoenix. You don't want those problems, and you know it." Nikki spat, then mugged him with intense anger.

He frowned. "Damn, TT, you turning on me, too?"

"Nall, but that's my baby, right there. His mama was my heart. You need to get your shit together, we'll get him right as well," Nikki said, getting up and opening the door for him.

Phoenix stepped out, looked into it and mugged me. "Nigga you better be ready to die for this shit. If you ain't, stay yo sheltered ass outta my way. I don't need you, fuck nigga. I got the streets of Tennessee all by myself." He stepped away from the door.

"You got three weeks, Phoenix. Three weeks to get your shit in order!" Shemar hollered. He closed the door and locked it. "Look, JaMichael, before you leave this office tonight, you gon' know everything you're supposed to know. You gotta remember you are in control of a lot of lives."

Nikki came up behind me and rubbed her hands over my shoulders. "Baby, we finna lace you, so get comfortable." She planted a soft kiss on my cheek.

I nodded. "A'ight fuck it, tell me everythang."

Chapter 6

A week later, and after being schooled by Shemar and Nikki every single day, I felt like I had a grand understanding of what was expected of me. Shemar and Nikki had already hired me a lethal security detail team that was bred by the slums of Cloverland. They were head bussas and pledged allegiance to me, by way of Shemar. Since I was a young, trigger happy, 'bout that life nigga, I wanted my Hittas to be the same way. I wanted young, starving savages that knew who fed them. I wanted killas I could eat off the same plate with. Muthafuckas that were bred in the projects and the gutters. All my soldiers had a reason to keep me breathing. They had a reason to protect me. The longer I kept breath in my lungs, the better the chances were at balling and living good. I didn't give a fuck if I was forced to work beside Phoenix or not. I wasn't fuckin' with the Duffel Bag Cartel. I formed my own Cartel of killas. I became the head of the Heartless Goons and had every intention of making sure my killas lived up to our name.

***

The first night I got back from Houston, Bubbie didn't speak two words to me. She simply walked up to me and handed me both of my sons. As soon as I felt them slide into my arms, my heart melted, and I felt so guilty for not being there on the days I had been in Houston. I kissed both of them on their little cheeks and held them as close to my heart as I could. They scrunched their faces and opened their eyes seemingly at the same time. The looks of them made me feel so weak. While I was bouncing them up and down, Bubbie appeared in the living room with a Birkin bag in her hands.

She grabbed the doorknob of the front door and pulled it open. "I'll see you in four days, JaMichael, bye."

"Wait, what?" I ran as fast as I could and caught her coming off the porch. It had just finished raining and the sun was just barely peeking from behind the clouds. "What you mean you finna be gone for four days?"

She chirped the alarm on her pink Mercedes Benz and opened the driver's door. "The way I see it. What's good for the goose is good for the gander."

I stood there looking dumbfounded for a second. "What the fuck is that supposed to mean?"

"It means you've taken three days away from this family doing only God knows what. So, I'm going to take an extra day because…well, kiss my ass." She sat in her driver's seat and slammed the door.

When she started the engine, she revved the engine three times before peeling backward. The screeching sound caused both twins to jerk and begin crying at the same time. She bellowed smoke from the tires and turned on to the street, before storming down it. She held her arm out the window with her middle finger up.

***

Danyelle came from the nursery and slowly pulled the door upward. She left it opened a crack. "You see, cuz, that's all we gotta do. All they need is a little tender, love, and care. She gon' be gone for four days but it's all good. We got this." She came, slid into my lap and wrapped her arms around my neck. "Now, if I wasn't mistaking, you said if I came over here and handled the boys, you would find time to handle me. Unfortunately, I'ma have to hold you to that." She leaned in and kissed my lips. Hers felt like soft pillows. I could both taste and smell the double mint gum she was chewing.

I tongued her ass down for about two minutes until my dick got hard as wood. She kept moving in my lap and moaning into my mouth. I stood up, and she stood right up with me and humped her pelvis into my front. She had on a thin Burberry sundress, so I could feel her heat easily. I cuffed her ass and picked her yellow ass up, then pressed her against the wall.

She locked her feet around my waist. "Please, JaMichael, fuck me. I'm begging you, I need some of this dick. It feels like it's been forever," she hissed and sucked hard on my neck.

She jumped down and started unbuckling my Ferragamo belt, lowering herself to her knees. As soon as my dick was free, she was all over it, hungrily. Sucking like her life depended on it.

I laid with my back against the wall and my fingers wrapped in a handful of her hair, humping into her mouth. The sounds of her gagging made me feel some type of way. That forbidden gene started coming full circle, by the time I was bending her thick ass over the couch, getting ready to slide inside of her, Jahliya, came through the door.

She stopped and dropped her Gucci bag right on the Welcome Mat. "What the fuck are y'all in here doing?" She snapped.

I jumped back with my piece bouncing up and down and scrambled to grab my boxers. Danyelle threw her dress over her head and pulled it down. Her nipples poked up against the dress and made her look so sexy. When she was dressed, she disappeared down the hallway without saying a word to Jahliya.

Jahliya walked right up to me, grabbed me by the throat, and pushed me back into the wall. "First you disappear on this girl for three days knowing she just got out of the hospital giving birth to your two kids. Then, as soon as you get back, you're in here fuckin', Danyelle? This damn thing is gon' get you in trouble." She grabbed my dick and held it firm in her small, right-hand, squeezing the life out of it. At least that's how it felt at first, but then for some reason, it started rising in her clutch. She frowned and pushed me back by use of it. "Boy, you crazy." She turned around and walked off.

"I already know that shit. I be trying like a ma'fucka to be cool, sis, but I'm addicted to pussy. It's too much of it out here. I can't focus long enough to stay away from it," I admitted, with my dick rock hard in front of me.

"Well, you gon have to get better control of yourself, Ja-Michael. I can see that you are killing yo' baby mama." She walked over to the couch and sat down, crossing her thighs.

I couldn't help but notice that her nipples were hard as hell, sticking through her Polo blouse. But they weren't that way when she'd first come into the house. I wondered if her grabbing my piece had done something to her sexually. Apart of me wanted to know I wasn't the only one with a problem like this. I felt so alone and helpless.

I came over and sat beside her. "Sis, I'm fuckin' up, and I know it, but I don't know what to do. I'm seriously addicted to pussy, I got a real problem."

"No, you don't, JaMichael. You just using that shit as an excuse to be a scrub like the rest of the dead beats all over the hood. Nigga, you're supposed to be better than that."

I shook my head. "Sis, I'm serious. Do you know I noticed that when you came in the house that at first, your nipples weren't hard, but as soon as you got done squeezing on my dick they were hard as a rock?"

She closed her eyes and crossed her thick thighs. "Shut up, JaMichael." She leaned back just a tad and the material of her blouse conformed around her areoles. They were dark brown. I could see them through the white materials and for some reason I got excited. She crossed her thighs again and her short skirt fell backward.

I could smell her perfume mixed with a hint of sweat. My eyes roamed over her thick frame, I felt so guilty. I reached and cuffed her right breast. At the same time, my hand went under her skirt. She opened her thighs and I felt her pussy lips through her panties. She was real hot down there. My dick started jumping in my boxers at the same time one of my sons started crying in the other room.

Suddenly she opened her eyes and pushed both of my hands away. "Uh-uh, JaMichael, you see that's yo' problem now." She stood up and ran her fingers through her hair.

"I got the baby, cuz!" Danyelle hollered.

"JaMichael, is it true that you had to get involved with the Cold Heart Cartel in order to get me free?"

I stood up. "I had to do what I had to do. The only way I was able to go at that nigga, Mikey's chin was if I got permission from Jefe' Pablo himself. Mikey represented a whole lot of money for him, in order for me to have been able to break that up, I had to promise him I would step in and handle the bidness Mikey used too. Now they pairing me with Phoenix and shit's just getting all out of whack."

Jahliya lowered her head. "I hate Phoenix just as much as I hated Mikey. Both of them ain't nothing but scumbags." She hugged herself and looked like she was about to cry.

I stepped over and pulled her into my arms. "What you saying, Jahliya? Did that nigga, Phoenix put his hands on you?"

She was quiet for a short time. "Don't worry about it, Ja-Michael. If Jefe' Pablo is saying you and him, have to work together, then that's what has to happen. You need to find a way to get along with him."

"Jahliya, that's not what I asked you. Did he put his filthy ass hands on you?"

She wiggled out of my embrace and turned her back to me. "Nikki said that if you make one wrong mistake they gon' kill our entire family with no regards. Is that true?"

I came around so I could stand in front of her again. I pulled her into my arms and held her. "I ain't scared of, Jefe' Pablo. I ain't scared of the Cold Heart Cartel. That shit don't put no fear in my heart. This Mexican, thinks he finna own me for the rest of my life. You know that shit ain't happening."

"What are you going to do then, JaMichael? Them Cartels run the whole South. There ain't nowhere we can run. They own everybody." She started to shake in my embrace. "I don't wanna go back through what I just came out of. I'd rather die than to go back through that shit. I swear to, Jehovah." Tears came from her eyes.

Seeing that crushed my soul, I hated when Jahliya cried. I hated it when Jahliya hurt. I grabbed her by her arms and looked into her beautiful face. "Sis, listen to me, I'ma figure this shit out. I promise you, I'ma figure this shit out. Then we gon' get the fuck up out of here."

"Where will we go, JaMichael? They are literally every-where. How will we make money?"

I shook my head. "I don't know, yet, but have faith. I will never fail you again, I promise."

She turned around to face me as tears ran down her cheeks. "I never did say thank you for not giving up on me, and for rescuing me." She sniffled. "I owe you my life, JaMichael. I really do." She stepped on her tippy toes and kissed my lips ever so softly. Then she wiggled her nose back and forth against mine.

I held her to me and rested my chin on the top of her head. "You should already know I will never give up on you. Every second you were gone I felt lost. You're all I need in this world, Jahliya. I don't love nobody as much as I love you."

She hugged my waist and took a step back, looking up at me. "JaMichael, as good as that sounds to me, I can't take that love from one of these lil' girls you are supposed to be rendering it to. You are my little brother and I love you to death. You have to believe that, but you have two baby mothers. You need to embrace one of them for the sake of your children." She stepped away from me and wound up in the kitchen with the refrigerator door open. "I'm hungry."

I stood there for a moment taking in the things she'd just said. I knew she was right, I had to buckle down and man up. I had to be there wholeheartedly for either Bubbie or Tamia.

I stepped into the kitchen and exhaled. "I want you to come see Pops with me."

She grabbed some lunch meat and washed her hands in the sink. Then she took a loaf of bread from the top of the refrigerator and proceeded to make herself a sandwich. "I don't know if I'm ready for that yet, JaMichael. I still hold a lot of ill will toward our father, especially since I really don't know what took place between him and my mother." She went back into the refrigerator and grabbed the American and Swiss cheese.

"Sis, then come see grandma down in Baton Rouge. She so crazy that she admitted to everythang. If you don't believe me, you can ask Bubbie. Pops didn't kill our mother's she did, because she crazy."

Jahliya spread a bunch of Mayonnaise on her sandwich, and cut it in half, then she slid the plate over to me. "Here, eat somethin'. You losing way too much weight, I don't like it."

I picked up the sandwich, took a bite out of it and chewed with my mouth open, smacking on purpose. "So, which one do you wanna holla at first?"

She shrugged her shoulders. "I don't know maybe, Taurus."

My eyes lit up. "When you wanna do this?"

"Whenever is fine, I just wanna get the shit out the way. I got some real tough questions for his ass, too. Questions that he better be ready to answer, or he will lose me for good."

Danyelle slid into the kitchen and lowered her head. She had her hands behind her back. "Jahliya, I hope you ain't mad at me for what you caught me and JaMichael doing? I ain't no ho or nothin', he the only dude I been with."

Jahliya kept chewing her food, instead of giving Danyelle a response, she bit off her sandwich again and chewed looking at her as if she were stupid. Danyelle musta got the hint, because she blushed and backed out of the kitchen. "JaMichael, when you get a chance. Can you and I have a talk, it's very important?" With those words, she left out of the room.

Jahliya rolled her eyes and looked at me with obvious disgust and anger. "I know she our family and all, but I can't stand her pretty ass. That bitch bet not have you catching no type of feelings for her, JaMichael. I swear to God, I'll kill you, and her," she said with her nostrils flaring.

I shook my head. "I don't love no female other than you. Don't get shit twisted, I'll be right back." I excused myself and met Danyelle in her room. She was sitting on the edge of the bed with her head down. I stepped into the room and closed the door. "Danyelle, what's good with you?"

She pointed at the dresser. "Go look."

I got up and walked over to her dresser. Directly on the top of it was a positive pregnancy test. I shot daggers at her. "What the fuck is this?"

"I ain't been feeling right for about a month. That's the tenth test in a row that came up positive. I think I need to go to the doctor like asap, but in order to, I need my medical card from my mother. Are you mad at me?"

I didn't know what to say. I looked at the pregnancy test again and sat on the bed beside her. I looked the test over again and felt sick to my stomach. "Ain't no sense for me to be mad at you. This is my fault, I should've known better. I'ma get your medical card from Veronica. Then we gon' find out what's going on. Now you sure I'm the only one you been with?"

She nodded. "Yeah."

I sighed and placed my arm around her. "Then we gon' figure this out together." I needed to get my shit together, that was for sure.

Ghost

Chapter 7

"A'ight, JaMichael, I know you don't really fuck wit' me like that, and I got ill feelings toward you as well, but we gotta get our ducks in a row. Or them Cold Heart Cartel niggas and them Sinaloas gon' start picking us off one by one. We gotta put our hatred to the side. The only way I see us being able to do this is right here in this ring," Phoenix said, leading the way into Tyson's Boxing Center.

He stopped at the desk where there were two older men with gray afros sitting behind it listening to the democratic debate.

"Mane, they gon' keep going at each other's head and Donald Trump gon' fuck around and be in the White House for a second term. When will these crazy Politicians learn?" the heavyset man said.

Instead of the slender, darker man responding, he stood up from his metal chair and clapped his hands together. "Now, I know that ain't, Phoenix? Is that my main man, right there?" He slapped his hands together again and cackled, then came around the table and he and Phoenix embraced.

Behind us were other boxers working a speed bag or punching on a punching bag while they worked their way around it so they could hit it from every angle. Some were jumping rope, while others were sparring in the ring. It smelled of Bengay and mint for some reason.

"Yeah, it's me, old-timer, I got some bidness I need to take care of. Me and my cousin got a few issues and we need to get it out of our system the Tyson way. When will the ring be open?"

The old man looked over at the ring then at Phoenix. "Say, young blood this is your district. I heard about what happened to yo' Potna, Mikey. Them dirty sons of bitches gunned him down like he wasn't shit right over there in Houston, filthy Texans. Well, you got my sincerest condolences." He patted Phoenix on the shoulder and took off toward the boxing ring. "Hey! Hey! Y'all get on up out of that rang. We got somebody important that need it, right now, so get!" he ordered.

The two sparring boxers looked down at him, then over at Phoenix. When they saw him, their eyes got as big as paper plates. One by one they made haste to get out of the ring, ducking under the ropes to do so.

The other heavy-set, older man came and handed us two pairs of boxing gloves, mouthpieces and a set of headgear. I waved off the headgear and began sliding my hands into the gloves one at a time. I couldn't wait to get my hands on Phoenix. I guess he musta thought it was sweet because he had me by about seven years, but I was getting ready to show his ass a thing or two. Once my gloves were on tight, after being assisted by the heavy-set, older man, I stepped into the ring and started bouncing up and down on my toes.

Phoenix slid into the ring and slammed his gloves together. He rolled his head around on his neck and pulled on the ropes. Then he was bouncing on his toes as well with a mug on his face. The gym doors opened and what seemed like a flood of people started to enter. They looked at the ring fascinated, before filling up the bleachers on each side of the ring. What struck me was the number of females that came inside. The dope boys seemed to gather on one side of the ring, while the trap girls gathered on the other. Music by *Moneybagg* began playing loudly, then I felt my heart pumping.

The slender older man, stepped into the ring with a newly adorned degree shirt on. "A'ight, y'all ready? Then bring ya asses over here," he ordered waving us over.

"Wait!" Nikki hollered, hurrying as cute as she could to the ring. She climbed the stairs and rested in my corner. "Y'all

bet not kill each other in there, I mean that shit. Now gone."
She waved us off with her hand.

The slender man brought us to the middle of the ring.
"Look, I don't know what's going on between you two, but
obviously you needed to come here to settle it. I wish that
more of our young folks took this approach. I want y'all to
keep it clean and listen to my commands. Touch gloves when
you're ready to get this thang on the road."

Phoenix held out his glove and I slapped it with mine, then
backed all the way into my corner. He laughed and nodded his
head. He bounced on his toes and settled into his corner.

"JaMichael, baby, I'm letting you know, right now, if he
starts fucking you up I'm popping his ass with no regard.
You're my lil' daddy, I ain't finna let nobody hurt you. I don't
give a damn what they talking about, come here." When I got
close enough she pulled me by the arm and kissed my cheek.
She smelled so good and I noticed a bunch of the trap girls
whispering amongst themselves, pointing at us. I didn't give a
fuck, Nikki was that deal to me.

"A'ight, let's get it on." The slender, older man announced.
He twirled his index finger in a circle to signal the bell.

Ding! Ding! Ding!

Phoenix came to the center of the ring with his face
guarded by his big boxing gloves. As soon as he got close
enough to me, he threw a jab and took a step back as if he were
feeling me out. I kept my gloves up, one protecting my chin
and my left hand ready to strike. I waited until he threw another jab and sidestepped him jabbing the quick times. He
blocked all three. The crowd began to cheer and encourage us
to fight. They seemed as if they were already bored by our
slow formalities.

Phoenix bounced up and down on his toes. "A'ight." He stepped forward and came at me quick, swinging fast and hard.

I caught four to the body and one to the jaw. None of his punches rocked me, but they were enough to let me know he meant business.

Nikki slapped the top of the buckle and balled up her fist. "Get his ass, baby. Get him!" She pointed at Phoenix.

I nodded and lowered my head, before rushing him and keeping my chin protected. As soon as I got close, I was blasting him with haymakers, all body shots, one after the other. *Right. Left. Right. Right. Left*, as hard as I could, right in the left rib cage.

He stood up on his tippy toes and winced in pain, before pushing me away with two hands. He laid against the ropes holding his ribs.

I backed up and looked him over. My adrenaline was pumping. I didn't give a fuck what was wrong with him. All I kept imagining and hearing in my mind was what Jahliya had hinted toward with him, and Mikey. I wanted to cause him as much pain as physically possible since Nikki and Shemar made it perfectly clear that I couldn't kill him.

He took a second to gather himself, mugged me and nodded. "A'ight den." He slammed his gloves together and came across the ring fast with his head low.

He rushed me and pushed me first, but not before I could blaze his ass in the jaw twice, one on each side. He shook it off and hit me with a three-hit combo. Two to the body and a tight hook across the jaw. I saw blue lightning and grew dazed for a minute. Before I could gather myself, he was on me again. This time with a four-hit combo. Two to the body, a left hook, and right cross into the face that sent me against the ropes.

60

I needed them to keep me on my feet. The crowd went crazy, the females were jumping up and down. The dope boys nodded and gave each other high fives. It was so loud in there I could barely hear myself think. Nikki remained quiet and kept her eyes pinned on me.

Phoenix looked over his shoulder at me with a smile, as he walked back to his side of the ring. I felt the blood oozing out of my nose and over my lips. I wiped it away with my glove and stood up. The stars disappeared, I came back to the center of the ring with my gloves raised, on shaky legs. Phoenix musta peeped this, because he smiled looking down at them and came back into the center ready to go.

The slender man waved his hand downward. "Fight."

Phoenix rushed me again, swinging hard and fast. This time I felt every punch he handed me. He caught me twice in the ribs, one on each side. Then he hit me with a right hook that twisted me and a left jab that sent me flailing back before he came with an uppercut that dropped me to one knee.

"Nigga!" he yelled. "You can't fuck wit' my bidness!"

The crowd was going crazy before, but now, they were out of their minds. I actually saw trap girls hugging each other as if they were celebrating his victory. The dope boys saluted Phoenix and laughed at me. When my eyes trailed up to where Nikki stood, once again, she hadn't taken her eyes off me.

She lowered her lids into slits. "Get yo' ass up lil' daddy. Get up before I fuck you."

I shook the cobwebs from my head. The older, slender man was counting, and I didn't even notice it. I heard him say the number seven before I bounced to my feet.

He took a hold of both of my boxing gloves and held them. "You a'ight, son, you wanna call the fight?"

I snatched my gloves away from him and pushed his ass. "Get the fuck out of my face." The crowd booed, loudly.

"Fight!" he ordered.

Phoenix rested on the ropes with his arms relaxed along them. He casually came back into this fighter's stance and came at me. I swung three times, he jumped back and charged me. He hit me with four hard blows in the face, pushed me and uppercut the shit out of me, so good that I spit my mouthpiece into the bleachers and fell.

Nikki came under the ropes and kneeled beside me, while the crowd went wild again. "Lil' Daddy, are you okay? Fuck this, you want me to pop his ass?" I could tell she was serious because her hand went inside of her Gucci purse.

While I could hear the questions, she was asking her audio sounded funny, as if it were muffled. My head was spinning, I felt like I wanted to throw up. I could feel blood dripping from my lips. Nikki wiped it away and smeared it across her skirt. "What do you wanna do?"

Behind her, Phoenix was already jacking with the dope boys and members of his Cartel. The females were taking pictures of him with their phones. He was posing and cheesing. He blew kisses at the crowd of females and nodded his head.

I thought about Jahliya and imagined him doing some sick shit to her, alongside Mikey, and my heart started beating fast. "Nikki, gon' back into my corner, Shawty, I got this nigga."

"JaMichael, fuck that. You don't got shit to prove. Fuck it, we can kill his ass later. Fuck, Jefe' Pablo, straight up lil' daddy."

I shook my head. "Just trust in me, gon' back over there."

She wiped more blood away with her thumb. "Okay." I could tell that she was worried. She didn't think I could whoop Phoenix, but I was sure I could. I had found the weakness in his fighting and I planned on using it against him.

I stood up and slammed my gloves together. "Let's go!"

Phoenix turned around. "Aw come on ref now that had to be more than ten seconds," he jacked.

The slender, older man waved his hand downward. "Fight!"

Phoenix sighed and turned all the way around. "Really?"

I threw up my guards, I could feel the blood from my nose dripping off my chin. I kept seeing Jahliya's face. I kept remembering how she looked laid up in that hospital bed for a month straight after I'd gotten her back. I felt my blood boiling.

Phoenix slowly came into the center of the ring, once again, as soon as he got close, he rushed me swinging hard. Instead of inhaling his blows, this time I took a big sidestep and rocked him with a right hook on the jaw. I saw sweat fly from the top of his waves. He wobbled and staggered, reaching out for the ropes. I didn't give him no time, I came full speed swinging only for his head region. I connected six times and pushed him into the ropes, before rocking him in the jaw again. He turned sideways and fell to the mat.

Nikko jumped up. "Hell yeah! Nigga, it ain't sweet! Fuck you thought this was!" she hollered.

The gym grew silent, they stood up and rubbernecked to get the best possible view of the ring. Phoenix struggled to come to his feet. He used the rope to come to a standstill. I didn't wait for the old dude to tell me shit. I rushed him again and started fucking him up blow after blow. He fell into my arms after the twelfth one, I scooped him and slammed him directly on his back. All I could see was my sister Jahliya's eyes with tears running out of them.

The slender man ran over and kneeled beside Phoenix. He looked him over and back at me. He seemed weary, then he was waving his hands through the air. "It's over, it's over!"

Nikko rushed into the ring up to me. She pulled my head down and kissed my lips. "I knew he couldn't fuck in yo' bidness, lil' daddy. Now he knows it, too." She hugged my neck. "Come on, let's get up out of here."

I got my stuff together and got out of the ring. The crowd had formed around the ring and as we were making our way out of the building, I noticed the dope boys mugging us. A few of them had their hands up their shirts as if they wanted to smoke me.

"I wish anyone of you lil' niggas would. I'll turn Memphis on its ass. Phoenix lost that shit fair and square, deal with it." She continued to pull my hand until we were out of the building and back into her Bentley Coupe.

"JaMichael, you gotta go home and get some rest. In two days, Jefe' Pablo, is sending you and Phoenix on y'all first mission to Milwaukee to take out a few members of the Sinaloa Cartel." She smiled and rubbed the side of my face. "I'm so glad you whooped his ass. Damn, I love me some you." She reached between my legs and grabbed my pipe.

Chapter 8

"So, what are we doing here, JaMichael? You think because you bringing me to some fuckin' State Fair it's gon' make everything right in our lives or something?" Bubbie rolled her eyes and crossed her arms in front of her.

I continued to count out a few gees and tucked the rest of the money I had on me into the seat of my Porsche? I wanted to make sure I had enough money so I could spoil her ass. I knew it wasn't going to be an easy task to get her back into a better space, but I was willing to do all I could to at least try.

"What you ignoring me now?" she asked, looking out of the window toward the gate where a throng of people was entering on the State Fairgrounds. It was nice and sunny, with just a hint of wind coming from the West.

"Nall, boo, I just feel like we need to take some time to rediscover each other again. I know I been fucking up and I ain't been on my game, but hopefully, we can start fresh, and make today day one." I stuffed the three gees into my pocket and turned to look at her.

The way I saw it, I had at least four to six hours to blow. I had already checked on all the traps and despite our fight the other day Phoenix was on top of the hustling side of things. He had Bandos jumping all over the state. I had to give him his props on that, as much as I hated the nigga.

"JaMichael, I'm so emotionally disconnected from you, right now, I don't know what to do. I feel like a tablet that's trying its best to connect to your Wi-Fi, but I'm not even picking up the signal. My heart, nor my mind won't even let me."

I understood. "I know, baby, but at least try for me. I'm going to give you my all from here on out, but you gotta give me a chance. Please?"

She sat there in the seat, with her arms crossed, looking out the window. "I don't want to be here right now. I feel very shitty. I'm missing my kids and I still ain't finished feeling out my forms so I can attend Memphis Area Technical College. They ain't gon' give me no more extensions."

"Bubbie, please baby, I just wanna spend some time with you. Can you please put that stubborn shit to the side for one day?"

She shot daggers at me with her eyes. "What?"

"I'm sorry, boo." I didn't want to irritate her further. It was best to just submit and tuck my tail. Whatever she says goes. Though I had a weakness for women, I loved the heaven out of Bubbie. And though my ways, more often than not, brought the hell out of her, she was truly my everything. "Please, baby, can daddy please spend some money on you? I just wanna see you smile, that's all." I leaned over and kissed her on the chin, then the side of the face. "Please."

She took a deep breath and exhaled loudly. "A'ight, come on den, but you gon' need a lot more than those few hunnit you just tucked away." She pushed me away and sat back in her seat. "I better have a good time, too. You already got two strikes."

I smiled, what else could I do?

***

We'd been kicking it around the park for about an hour when Bubbie wanted to go on the Ferris Wheel. After standing in line for ten minutes we were finally aboard the ride. It made a full revolution, then she cleared her throat. "JaMichael, what makes men cheat so much?"

I was sipping on a Sprite through a straw, her question damn near made me spit all my pop out. It went down the wrong pipe, I started coughing. She was so broken, she didn't even bother hitting me on the back. I cleared my throat and got myself together. "Baby, where is this coming from?"

She mugged me. "Do we even have to go there?" She flared her nostrils and looked off. It was starting to get a lil' dark and the Fair was beginning to look all cool and shit because of all of the colorful lights.

"Baby, you wanna know what's crazy?"

"What?" she asked, dryly.

"When it comes to most men, well, let me just speak for myself in general. I don't really feel like I'm cheating if I smash a nobody ass bitch because it's like she don't mean nothing to me. It's more of a curiosity thang. A man can look at a woman, the way she is built, the way she talks, or acts and just start to wonder what it would feel like to fuck her. It's as simple as that. Then once he finds out she becomes irrelevant. We can literally go on about our days and never think twice about that bitch again unless we see her in traffic."

"Sooo, you think it's cool to jeopardize me and your sons because you're curious to know what it'll feel like to be with some random bitch, really? How much sense does that make?"

'*Here we go*,' I thought. "Nall, I don't mean it like that."

"But it's just what you said."

"That's not what I said. There you go twisting shit around again." I was starting to get irritated.

"Nall, there I go calling you on your selfish, immature bullshit. You got a whole ass family, but you think it's cool to be out here fucking these, nasty ass jump-offs? JaMichael, I swear to God if you bring me something from one of those nasty bitches, I'ma shoot you straight in the face with my gun and I'ma leave yo ass right there and go about my day. I'm not gon' even think about you again until I see you in traffic. Yo' sick ass. Ugh, I can't believe I fell for yo' ass." She leaned against me and pushed off. "Get the fuck off me."

I took my arm from around her, as the Ferris Wheel reached its highest point and made its way around again. We were silent for a while. I was wishing I had never brought her ass out. I could've been trapping right alongside Phoenix, or with my Heartless Goon crew. I didn't feel like arguing wit' Bubbie.

"Even though you treat me like shit. Even though, you cheat. Even though you fuckin' that Danyelle bitch, who is your fuckin' cousin, I still allow it, I still stand by yo' triflin' ass, and I still remain faithful to you. Whenever a bitch is as stupid as I am, they don't deserve nothing other than the heart-ache and pain they are already gettin'." She lowered her head. "Why the fuck do I love you so much? You ain't even about shit."

I couldn't say nothing. I was sitting beside a woman I had broken. Bubbie was a fresh eighteen, not even two months in and already she was speaking like a woman in her thirties. "Bubbie, the only thing I can say is that I'm sorry."

"That's what you always say, JaMichael. You always say you're sorry, but you never say for what, or that you are sure it will never happen again. You know why you don't say the last part? I'll tell you why. It's because you know you will do it again and you know I'll let yo' triflin' ass do it and get away with it. Why? Because I'm weak." She frowned her face. "I am eighteen with two kids and a baby father that runs the streets all day and night. My mother distancing herself from me, and my father don't even wanna talk to me. What the fuck am I even here for, seriously?"

The Ferris Wheel slowly came around and we were helped off the ride. Bubbie took off walking fast as soon as her feet hit the pavement. She wiped tears from her cheeks.

I jogged to catch up. "Baby, can you please slow down?"

She kept speed walking. "What for, JaMichael? I'm lost right now and you ain't givin' me no clarity. I feel like a walking corpse. You wanna know what's fucked up? Every time I look at JaMichael and KaMichael, I start to love them less because they look so much like yo' ass. I pray they don't turn into the man you've become." Now she was really crying. She took off running through the Fair, bumping people out of the way.

I took off running behind her. She zig-zagged and squeezed through the tightest crowds. She wound up running into the Women's bathroom, into a stall slamming and locking it. I ran in right behind her. When I got inside, I saw that there were about six women inside washing their hands. When they saw me, they looked baffled and rushed out of the bathroom.

I walked down the row of stalls until I was standing outside of Bubbie's. "Baby, please don't do this, right now. I love you, now come out here so we can talk."

A toilet flushed, the lock to a stall clicked and a small white girl with blond hair appeared. She placed the strap to her purse over her shoulder. "Hey, you're not supposed to be in here—it's, for girls only."

"I know, but I'm dealing with an emergency. All I need is five minutes. Bubbie, come out baby."

The white girl stayed poised. "Girls only means, no seconds, I'm going to get security." She walked right out of the bathroom without washing her hands. *Nasty ass.*

"Bubbie, get yo' ass out here before you get me locked up."

"Good, at least while yo' ass is locked up you can't cheat on me wit' a million bitches." She kicked the stall's door. "I hate you, Ghost! I wish I never detested that bitch Tamia so much. If I hadn't, I would have never gone after yo' ass! This is what the fuck I get!" she screamed.

That little bit of reality smacked me hard. I had always thought the only reason Bubbie was on my heels was because of her hatred toward Tamia. Tamia had been something like my high school sweetheart. Bubbie had been her rival since elementary. Somehow along the way, Bubbie and I wound up together and the rest is history.

"Bubbie, this bitch just said she finna go and get the police. Now you know I'm ridin' dirty. I got two .40s on me. Bring yo' ass out of that stall before you get me popped off!"

She clicked the lock and slammed the door open. "Fine, but I still hate yo' ass! You screwed up my life—and give me my shit!" She bumped me out of the way and snatched the big teddy bear I'd won her at the basketball shooting game, out of my hand.

I stood there for a second trying my best to collect myself, then followed her out of the bathroom. She stopped at the entrance and lowered her Chanel sunglasses, peering out into the distance. "Shit, here we go."

I stepped up beside her and tried to see what she was looking at. "What?"

"JaMichael, I already heard from somebody that ain't yo' bidness, about that deal you had to make in order to get your sister back. You ain't been in this bullshit long enough to know when to spot those Sinaloa ma'fuckas, but I can. If you look straight ahead right by that trailer selling pizza, you finna see two Mexican looking cowboys with big belt buckles and a black bandanna around their neck. They are Sinaloas."

I looked straight ahead and saw what she was talking about right away. "Fuck." I looked from left to right and saw that the Fair was packed. There was no way they would attempt to do anything stupid while all these people were around. I was sure of it. "A'ight, we gotta ease up outta here and get back to the car. Once we get there, I can lose their asses. That Porsche hit way over a hunnit."

Bubbie nodded. "Well, it ain't just them two over by the Pizza stand. It's those two by the water boats and three over there by the Bumper cars. How the fuck we finna shake all of them?"

I felt like I had a shortness of breath. I thought about grabbing one of the .40s off my hip and going Kamikaze, but that would have been stupid. There was a good chance the police would gun my ass down well before the Sinaloas had a chance to do it. "Damn, damn, damn. What the fuck do we do?"

Bubbie looked over her shoulder. "We could climb out of that window, right there. It leads to the parking lot. Then we just gon' have to make a run for it." She hugged her bear close. "Can't forget this."

I jogged over to the window, raised it, hopped up on the ledge and looked out of it. There didn't appear to be any one of the enemies surrounding the parking lot. There was just one security man in a yellow vest. A heavy-set white dude, he appeared harmless. "Baby fuck that bear, I'll get you another one."

"Hell n'all, I'm taking my bear with me. This is the nicest thing you've done for me in a long time." She tucked the bear under her arm and came to stand beside me as I stepped on my tippy toes and looked out of the window again.

I looked down at her. "Bubbie, that bear just gon' slow you down lil' mama. I promise I'll get you another one. Now come on, you're going through first." I held out my hand for her.

She smacked it away. "JaMichael, if you say one more thing to me about me leaving my bear, we're about to have a serious problem. You ain't finna have to worry about those

Sinaloas getting all up in your ass because I'ma get there first. Now move." She stuffed the Jumbo-sized bear into her bag as good as she could, then lifted her foot into my hand. I hoisted her upward. As soon as she got on to the ledge and half of her body through the window, she dropped both her purse and the bear. Her strapped had completely broken. "JaMichael." She stuck her head through the window and pointed down at it.

I leaned over to pick it up, as soon as I did the bathroom door slammed open. I heard footsteps and looked behind, just as four of the Sinaloas were rushing into the bathroom. One of them aimed his gun that had a silencer attached and fired.

Chapter 9

Big chunks of the bathroom wall exploded right on the side of my head. "Shit!"

I slung the bear, and Bubbie's purse through the window to her, before I jumped up, and wiggled way through it. Another shot was fired shattering the window as I fell on my back.

Bubbie and I took off running in the direction of the parking lot. The sun had completely gone down. Now the Fair was lit up colorful and the sounds of it resonated all the way to the back of the event where we were. I could hear bullets whizzing past our heads. Bubbie dropped the bear again; I stopped and picked it up as bullets ate at the gravel around me trying my best to catch up to her. Bubbie kicked off her wedged sandals and really started booking it. By the time we reached the parking lot, the Sinaloas were no longer chasing us. We jumped into my Porsche and I sped away, kicking dust in the air.

***

Later that night, as I laid on my back with a million thoughts running through my mind, Bubbie came to the doorway of our bedroom and exhaled. She entered the room and kneeled on the bed, then crawled across it, and laid beside me with her arm draped across my body. "Hey, Daddy, what you up doing?"

"That shit from earlier still going through my head. This game is getting the better of me already, Bubbie, and it's just beginning. I got a long way to go; this shit is stressful."

She maneuvered her body so that she was laying her head on my chest. For some reason, she had a thing for listening to my heartbeat. Once she had her ear positioned right, she began to rub my stomach muscles. "JaMichael, who's to say we have to live this life? Why can't we run away from them? Why can't we find a better life somewhere away from Memphis? It ain't like we don't have the means to do so."

Moneybagg continued playing low from the speakers that were hung in each corner of our room. Whenever I started stressing, for some reason listening to the homie allowed me to get peace of mind. "Baby, you should already know it don't work like that. The Cartels run the world. It ain't nowhere I could go where, Jefe' Pablo or his henchmen wouldn't find me. Ain't no way out of this shit, it's til' the death."

Bubbie sat up and ran her fingers through her curly hair. She sucked on her bottom lip, then frowned. "JaMichael, you don't got no time to be dying for some fuckin' Cartel. You got two lil' boys to worry about now and me."

"I know that already, Bubbie. Damn, why would you bring up the obvious?" I said irritated.

"Because not one time have you mentioned us. It's been you, you, you. New flash, once those babies were born, it is no longer about you. It should be about them first, then me, and then you. That's how it's supposed to go."

I pulled back the blankets and sat on the edge of the bed. "As long as this Jefe' Pablo dude got me as part of his workers, I ain't got no family. Because admitting I have a family means I'm admitting that when he kills me, he's coming to kill y'all too. As long as I'm speaking like I'm the only one that's wrapped up in this shit, that's how it'll be."

Bubbie picked up a pillow and swung it as hard as she could. She bonked me right on the side of the head and it rocked me for a second. Then she was standing right in my face, all five-feet-four inches of her, with her fists balled.

"Nigga you sound so fucking stupid and so fuckin' weak. Ugh, who are you?" She poked her finger to my forehead and pushed it like I was a punk or something.

I stood up and grabbed her by her shoulders. "Shawty watch yo' ma'fuckin' mouth and fall yo' lil' ass back before I choke you out."

She smacked her lips and waved me off. "Nall fuck that. How the hell are you going to let somebody punk you, huh? How you gon' let some nigga all the way in Mexico call shots over you? Use and abuse you until he's done with you, and as soon as he is done, he ain't gon do shit but put a bullet in your head."

"Shawty, I ain't tryna do this, right now." I went to side-step her.

She grabbed be by the straps of my tank-top and pulled me back in front of her. I could hear the material of my shirt stretching. "Nigga, I don' gave yo' ass two beautiful little boys. You finna stand here and talk this shit out until we get an understanding because I don't like what I'm seeing. It's making me sick on the stomach. Now, what are you going to do?" She asked looking up to me with seething anger.

I didn't know what to do, in my mind Jefe' Pablo had me by the balls. He was too powerful. He was connected all over America, and all it would take was one word from him, my life and all the lives of those I love, would be taken. I felt like it was my best bet to just follow his commands and stay alive for as long as I could. I didn't see any other options, but the look on Bubbie's face told me I wasn't doing something right.

"Baby, instead of me coming up with some shit that's gon' only piss you off even more. Why don't you tell me what I should be doing?"

"JaMichael, you fight, fuck dude. Boy, ain't no pussy in you or on you. You are young, but you're all man. Look at you and you got all this dick." She cuffed it and held onto my shit. "Ain't no pussy in you. If that ma'fucka wanna try and treat you like a bitch, then you play yo' role until you can outsmart him. As soon as you figure out how to penetrate his circle, you get in and body his ass. The body can't function without the head. You feel me?"

I nodded. "Yeah, Boo, I do."

She released my dick, I guessed because it started to get hard in her hand. "Dang, you always getting hard, ain't he tired of fuckin'?"

"Nope, bring yo' lil' ass over here." I pulled her to me, even though, she was trying to fight me off most of the way.

"Stop, get off me, JaMichael, dang."

Once I had my big arms wrapped around her, I knew there was nothing she could do. "I looked into her pretty eyes and for the first time, I saw something different. I saw my strength, I saw my courage, I saw my purpose. My strongest and best half. "Bubbie, I'm sorry for not being the man I'm supposed to be to you."

She continued looking into my eyes. "Are you really, now?"

"Baby, listen to me because I'm serious. I wanna sincerely apologize, as a man."

She wiggled out of my embrace and pushed me off her. "JaMichael, I don't wanna hear none of that sentimental shit? You ain't gon' do nothing but apologize to me like you always do, then you gon' wind up going right back to doing the shit you been doing. You wanna apologize to me? How about you apologize with actions, instead of words?" She picked the pillow up off the floor that she'd hit me with.

When she did her nightgown rose and I saw that she wasn't wearing no panties. I hadn't gotten the chance to hit them goodies ever since she'd given birth to our children, and I was missing it.

"So, what you saying, you ain't got no faith in me?"

"Nope, I understand your nature, which is to be a ho. That's just what you are. As soon as you recognize that, you'll be able to make peace with yourself. I mean, I already have. I can never see you as my husband because I can't trust yo' ass. You're triflin', which means I can go about this one of two ways; I can either accept how you are and wrap my future around you, or I can follow my Bible and find my children a real man. So, that they can have a father and a mother who are married and living under a kingdom household. I'm lettin' you know right now, I am leaning toward the latter."

I closed in the distance between us so fast I didn't know I did it until I was in her face. I grabbed her by the neck and held her up against the wall, pinning her. She struggled to break free but wasn't nothing happening. I leaned into her ear. "Bubbie, if you ever say anything like that to me again, I swear on my twins, I will fuck you up. If you ever think you gon' have another nigga playin' daddy to my shawties, you got another thang coming lil' one. I'll smoke that nigga like barbeque, then leave yo ass somewhere twisted. You and those boys belong to me. I'm lettin' you know that shit, right now. Do you understand that?"

She looked into my eyes without blinking. Then with all her might, she uppercut me as hard as she could right in the stomach. I expelled a gasp of air. She used that distraction to push me as hard as she could. I flew into the wall. "Nigga, fuck what you talking about. I carried those boys, I was in labor with them for damn near two days. You don't tell me what to do with them, or me. If you wanna be a part of me and my sons' lives, then earn it. You earn the right to be my husband and you earn the right to be their role model. And don't you ever put your fuckin' hands on me again. I am their mother!" she screamed.

I stood mugging her, I wanted to kick her ass. I wanted to snatch her up and verbally chew her out, but how could I when she was spitting the truth, standing firm on her square as a woman? I had more respect for her than anything. "Bubbie, I'm sorry."

She pointed toward the door. "Get the fuck out of this room, JaMichael."

"Bubbie, get off that bullshit." I took a step toward her. "Come here lil' mama."

She balled up her fists and held them on the sides of her face like a boxer. "We finna fight if you try and touch me again, JaMichael, get the fuck out of this room, now!"

I stood there for a second with a dumb ass look on my face. Then I waved her off. "A'ight, well fuck you then. You always on this bullshit." I snatched a pillow off the bed and threw it at her ass. Fuck you, Bubbie." I turned to leave out of the room.

"You never fight for me, JaMichael," she whimpered. "You always leaving. You don't give a fuck about me and I'm sick of it, I'm so tired." She fell to her knees and grabbed the bear that I'd won her at the Fair. She wrapped her arms around it and hugged it as tight as she could while tears leaked out of her eyes.

I stopped in my tracks and felt like I was going to be sick. "Bubbie, baby, please tell me what you want me to do?"

She shook her head. "You're supposed to just know, JaMichael, you're the man. All I know is that you are killing me. You're breaking my little heart. I don't know how much more of this I can take without losing my mind." She squeezed her eyelids together, then our boys started crying in the nursery room next door. It was as if they could feel their mother hurting.

I kneeled and hugged her frame. "I swear to God, I love you, Bubbie. I will do anything for you. You gotta believe that, mama. I ain't got it all figured out, I wish I did, but I don't. Can you cut me some slack?"

She cried harder into the teddy bear. "JaMichael, you have a family now. Having a family means no slack. You gotta be on your A-game, it's as simple as that. All our lives are on the line. You have to be our saving grace and saving our family starts with you and me." She stood up and wiped her face with the back of her hand. "I'm leaving you, JaMichael."

"What?"

She sniffled, wiped her tears again, walked over to the nightstand and pulled out a calendar. She slammed it on top of the dressers and pointed at it. "Today is September first, I am giving you until October first to get your shit together. That is one month from today. After that month is concluded, you need to only be about me and your children, our family! Squash this Cartel shit, squash this shit with, Tamia and Danyelle, and whoever. On October first you are to only be about me and your sons. Do you understand that?"

I did. "Yeah, but where are you going until then?"

"I'm going to my mother's mansion and trust me, I'll be counting down the days until you come for me? What you have to realize, JaMichael is that I love you more than life itself. Something deep within my soul wants us to make it. I know you were created for me and what's crazy is that I can't even tell you why I know that. However, I feel it so deeply in my heart." She poked my chest. "But you have to get your shit together. You're failing me. So, can we agree on a month?"

I nodded and pulled her to me. I wrapped her in my embrace. "Yeah, boo, I'm coming for you at that time. I promise to have all this shit out of my system. I love you, please never forget that." I kissed the top of her head.

"Don't tell me nothing about love, JaMichael, show me."

Chapter 10

Phoenix took a sip from his glass of Jack Daniels and burped into his fist. He wiped his mouth with the back of his hand. "Man, I ain't been back home since I was about fourteen years old. It feels real good to be back, especially on bidness." He picked the glass up again and downed the rest of the contents.

We were in a small cafe, there were about fifteen tables and the menu consisted mostly of easy to make food: Burgers, French Fries, Ham sandwiches and things of that nature. I had just eaten half of a burger and was good to go. I was Leaning and had popped a few Purks. My body felt breezy and my eyes were lower than hell.

"Mane, we been sitting at this ma'fuckin' table for an hour like we on some kind of date or something, nigga. What the fuck is the holdup?" I asked, looking across the table at him.

He pulled his nose, his eyes seemed to be lower than mine. He'd tooted two grams of Tar before we even stepped foot in Phoenix, Arizona. "Mane, you, already—know—" He dozed off and started scratching himself. Then came back to about five seconds later. "How—long—this shit takes." He ran his hand over his face, exhaled, blinked like three times, then bucked his eyes as far open as they could go.

"What the fuck are we waiting on?" I wanted to know looking around, scanning the restaurant.

He took a sip from the ice water he had on the table, dipped his fingers inside of it and ran them along the jugular vein of his neck, I imagine to cool himself off. I had visions of slicing his throat. I hated this nigga, I didn't give a fuck if he did have my blood running through him.

He sat upright. "We waiting on—" He blinked twice and swallowed his spit. "That Mexican bitch right there gon' give me the signal when it's time to go up there, and handle bidness." He wiped his mouth again. "Jefe' Pablo heard about how them Sinaloa ma'fuckas tried to get at you, he wants us to make a big splash. That's the way this game go. When they come at us, we supposed to come back at them ten times harder. Kill or be killed."

I eyed the Mexican chick from across the room. She was short, with silky black hair. She had a pretty face and some weight on her that didn't look bad at all. As soon as I started imagining what it would be like to fuck her from the back, I saw Bubbie in my mind and I shook that image of sexually slaying the Spanish chick out of my head.

"Nigga, you talking like you actually got a stake in Jefe' Pablo's Cartel. You ain't shit but a temporary worker just like the rest of us."

"Yeah, well, if it's one thing I learned about Jefe' Pablo, it's that as long as you're doing yo' job, he gon' make sure you get rich and your life is long lasting. It ain't until you fall off and become a problem that he seeks to get rid of yo' ass. As long as I'm part of the Cold Heart Cartel, the Duffel Bag Cartel, under me will be prosperous." He pulled out a cigarette and lit the tip.

I backed up and fanned my face. "Don't blow that stanking ass shit over here." I hated the smell of cigarettes.

He frowned and blew the smoke to the ceiling. "Dawg, you need to ease up with your animosity toward me. I ain't have shit to do with what Mikey did to your sister. Had I known that fuck nigga even had that in mind, or that you and Jahliya was my blood, I woulda laced that nigga a long time ago. Mikey ain't been right ever since we formed that Cartel."

I eyed him from across the table. "Nigga, birds of a feather."

"Nall cuz, that's where you wrong. Me and that bitch nigga wasn't nothing alike. He did his thing, I did mine. He was supposed to run Black Haven and I was supposed to run Orange Mound. Whatever he was doing over there was of no concern to me, just as long as when he came to the table at the end of the week, he had the amount of money he was supposed to have." Phoenix assured me. His speech was getting better. It sounded like the dope was either wearing off or he was getting better control of it.

"Well, I been in Memphis for as long as I can remember and as long as I been here you and Mikey been thick ass thieves. The whole city already knew that when they saw you, they saw Mikey, and vice versa. You had to have known he was finna kidnap my sister and you had to have known where she was all this time. I ain't buying this blond ignorance you're selling. Stop feeding me bullshit. We got a job to do. Let's focus on doing that before me and you wind up tearing this ma'fucka up." I could feel my heart beating like crazy in my chest. I knew that was a sign that I was seconds away from flying off the deep end.

"Cuz, what the fuck you want from me? Nigga, we supposed to be family. All that hatred we had for each other before we found out we were related needs to go out the window. I got your back from here on out and you got mine, it's as simple as that," Phoenix said, slightly slurring his words.

I eyed him and looked off. "If I ever find out you hurt my sister, I'm smoking you. Mark my words!"

He mugged me with his nostrils flared, then nodded. "Yeah, a'ight Phoenix. I see how this shit finna work, it's all good. From here on out we just do the job, Jefe' Pablo assigning us to do and that's that. I'll keep making sure we're meeting that financial quota. You just keep on doing whatever the fuck it is that you do, which is nothing, with the exception of being Taurus's son." He laughed and beat his fist on the table. "I got the streets, bitch nigga, I am the slums."

I ran my tongue across my teeth. "When we finish this job, fuck nigga, I'm taking over Orange Mound. You gon' take all them Duffel Bag niggas and move them to Black Haven with you. Orange Mound officially belongs to the Heartless Goons and we can cement that takeover, however, the fuck y'all want too. Nigga when you move, be sure to tell yo' niggas that Ghost has spoken."

Phoenix was quiet, just mugging me. His cigarette had ashes that were piled up as high as a top fade. He hadn't taken a pull off it in that long. "JaMichael, if we start warring with each other, Jefe' Pablo, is going to kill both of us because we will pose a threat to his Enterprise. It's best for us to get an understanding amongst ourselves."

"Orange Mound is mine," I said through clenched teeth. "Fuck Jefe' Pablo and fuck you Duffel Bag, niggas. Bitch, I'm, Ghost! What?" My hands were resting on the handles of my twin .40s. If Phoenix said anything out of the ordinary, I was getting ready to light his ass up with no remorse.

The Mexican chick came to the table with a tray of food in her hands. She sat a basket of French Fries on the table and it had a pair of keys on top of it. Her perfume smelled loud and cheap. I didn't like it. "Here you go sir, you gentlemen call me if you need anything else." She sashayed away from the table, with her mediocre ass swaying from left to right. I wasn't impressed.

Phoenix slipped the keys from the French Fries and tucked them into his pocket. "Come on, it's time to body these niggas. This shit gotta be gruesome, I hope you got it in you." He slid from the booth and grabbed his jacket.

**

Phoenix fit one of the keys into the lock of the side door of the restaurant and pushed it open. He stepped aside and allowed me to enter the dark hallway alongside him. As soon as I was inside, he closed the door back softly, placed the bag he was carrying on the ground, and pulled a ski mask out of his waistband. After pulling it over his head, he nodded with his head up the stairs.

I secured my mask and pulled my silenced .40 from my waist. I took the steps two at a time. When I got to the top, Phoenix stepped in front of me and slid the second key into the lock. He opened the door and moved inside the apartment. It was eleven o'clock at night. The house smelled like Bacon and Meth smoke. I eased inside with my gun held out in front of me.

"Bruh, remember you shooting to maim. We gon' kill them with this shit we got in this bag. Jefe' Pablo wants his shit recorded."

I nodded and put some pep in my step. I could hear murmuring toward the kitchen, so I made my way in that direction. Before I could get that far, I saw two Mexican dudes in the living room with a brick of Meth in front of them. They were bagging it up with their heads down and doctor's masks covering their faces. I aimed and fired two shots at the one closest to me, as Phoenix rushed past me into the kitchen. My target flew back holding his shoulder. He hollered out in pain. I fired again, knocking a chunk out of his other shoulder. Now he was writhing in pain, with blood gushing out of him.

His partner ran to the couch and tried to flip it over. I rushed him firing. The first slug hit him in the back. He fell on top of the couch. The second slug punched a hole in his temple and knocked his noodles out the other side of his head. He laid over the couch shaking. The first target tried to get up, he hugged himself and made a run for the door. I caught him in the knee with a slug. He buckled, his knee blew off his leg and twisted him on his back. He groaned like a wounded bear.

I locked the door and peeked toward the kitchen. It lit up eight times by gunfire. I heard the table being flipped over and a bunch of scurrying around. I wondered if Phoenix needed help. I was hoping the enemy had already killed him. That brought a smile to my face. About thirty seconds later that smile disappeared. Phoenix came trotting down the dark hallway with his chest heaving up and down.

***

I kneeled down and pulled on the man's ear, before slicing it off and tossing it on his chest. Phoenix held the phone and recorded me stride for stride. "What the fuck all he wants me to do?" I asked.

"You just gotta fuck dude over. If you want me to demonstrate, I ain't got no problem with that."

I waved his ass off. "I got this."

The man under me had his mouth duct-taped. He laid still with sweat pouring down his forehead and blood coming from the portion of his left ear that was still attached to his face. He groaned into the tape and started to shake. To the right of him were six other men duct-taped and tied the same as he was.

"Get his ass nigga. What the fuck is you waiting on?" Phoenix snapped. "We ain't got all day, imagine that fool is me."

I laughed at that and curled my lip under the mask. Then I raised the knife over my head and brought it down with a fury. The blade plunged into his soft flesh and split it. Blood seeped out of his wound and bubbled over his mug. I raised it, again and again, going nuts on him. He began kicking his legs, then he was shaking. I kept stabbing until he laid still.

Phoenix took his eyes away from the camera and bucked his eyes in his mask. He looked the man over and nodded. "Fuck, yeah, a'ight, let me handle my bidness for Jefe' Pablo too."

I ignored him, instead of releasing the serrated Hunter's knife to him, I went berserk, and worked my way down the line, slaying one man after the next. I literally blacked out for a full three minutes. When I came back to the living room was a sea of red and there were six lifeless bodies laid before me. The sleeve of my black long shirt was drenched in blood. I couldn't believe what I'd just done. I felt light-headed and out of my mind.

Phoenix recorded everything, then turned the camera to himself, and spoke through his mask. "Viva Cold Heart." He clicked off the camera and slid the phone into his pocket. "A'ight, let's get the fuck up out of here."

Ghost

Chapter 11

A week later, Phoenix and his Duffel Bag Cartel crew were having a cookout, at Washington Park, when me, Shemar, and thirty of my Heartless Goon Cartel killas pulled up in black vans and jumped out on them. We were all dressed in fatigues, black boots, and leather gloves, with black bandannas around our necks. Phoenix was sitting at this picnic table with his baby mother, Alicia the bitch who had once been Mikey's wife, when he saw me, he jumped up. He met me halfway.

I stepped in his face. "Nigga, yo' times up. We moving into Orange Mound today, one way or the other."

"Seriously, JaMichael, you finna do this shit, right here while all my people are watching?"

I shrugged my shoulders. "I told you a week. It's been a week, today is the day. You need to pack up yo' hittas and y'all gotta go. We ready to set up shop."

Phoenix looked behind him, all his Duffel Bag Cartel killas were standing up with their hands under their shirts. They looked like they were ready for him to give them the order to jump a war off. "Look, JaMichael, we celebrating my nigga's release from prison. Let us finish this lil' get together and we'll move the troops out tomorrow. How does that sound?"

"Sound like we about to shoot you niggas the fuck up. That's what it sounds like to me." I pulled my Glock from my waistband.

All my killas behind me upped their fully automatics and cocked them, bitches. They spread out and per my orders previously, blocked each exit of the park. We weren't letting nobody out of the vicinity. I wasn't playin' with these Duffel Bag niggas, fuck that.

The crowd began to murmur in worry. Phoenix's men looked like they didn't know what to do. They upped their guns and he put up a hand halting them.

"Wait." He looked into my eyes. "Y'all put that shit away. These are our brothers. We are going to give them Orange Mound because they run under my cousin, JaMichael, here and we are blood." He looked at me from the corners of his eyes.

I knew he was trying to save face, I didn't give a fuck what he had to do as long as in the end, I was moving into Orange Mound, with my Goons. I was tired of living in my father Taurus's shadow. I had to establish my own throne in the streets and my own legacy. I looked over my shoulder at my soldiers, they were ready to go. I had already told them we ain't come over here for talking or negotiations and I meant that.

"Check this out, we about to roll down to the projects and start kicking in doors and putting muthafuckas out. The Swine that work that beat been paid off, they gave us six hours to do what we need to do. So, basically, we can do this shit the smooth way or we can do this the bloody way. It's whatever you wanna do. You got an hour." I looked into his eyes and dared him to get stupid before I turned my back on him. I paused, "Oh and from here on out nigga don't call me by my Government, my muthafuckin' name is, Ghost."

Shemar nodded at me, we turned and left Phoenix standing there looking like a damn fool.

An hour later, me and my crew were moving into Orange Mound. All the traps where he and his Hittas used to reside were turned into our spots. All the people that seemed like they had a problem with our transition were put the fuck out? I literally had my soldiers knocking on one door at a time asking the residents if they had a problem with me, Ghost taking over Orange Mound. Those muthafuckas that hesitated were tossed out on their ass and that was that. I was tired of being nice and tired of cutting ma'fucka's slack. Nall, I didn't know how much time I had left on earth, but before I went, I wanted to be a bigger legend than my father, Taurus. We set up shop that night and extended our arms to all the dope heads in the area by giving them a hit for free and letting them know Orange Mound was under new management. I made sure the batch gave away was every bit of seventy percent, which in the heroin world was enough to get the hypes talking and having long conversations about their loyalty.

Three days after we took over Orange Mound, I threw a huge cookout and invited all the families that lived on my newfound turf. I'd posted signs everywhere and made it clear that it was free and that I didn't want them to bring nothin'. The cookout was set to be nothing more than a meet and greet and a way for me to extend my hand to the community I owned.

I sat back in the midst of the cookout, with two, six-feet-five-inch, three hundred plus pound, bodyguards standing behind me, heavily armed. I had another hitta in a parked car watching me from a distance, and four more peeking out of the project windows looking for anything out the ordinary. There were eight more on foot patrolling the area outside the cookout and two vans of killas rolling up and down the strip that led into Orange Mound. This shit was serious, I was starting to feel like a boss, and I knew the protection was very much needed. I had a feeling, Phoenix had some dirty shit up his sleeve, and that the Sinaloas wasn't that far away from me looking for a route to attack.

***

The night of the cookout, I showed up unannounced to Yvonne, Bubbie's mother's house to see if I could just see my baby mother. I had been on that killa shit all day long and now I was feeling like I just wanted to see her so I could tune into my emotions a lil' bit. After knocking for a few moments, Yvonne answered the door, rocking a nice Burberry outfit, with the matching purse in her hand.

When she saw me, she sighed and crossed her arms in front of her. "What do you want."

I grabbed her and kissed her, first on one cheek, then the other, before releasing her from my hold. She blushed and bucked her eyes. "Go tell Bubbie I need to see her, and these are for you." I picked up the Louis bag to the right of me and handed her a bouquet of red roses.

She took them, sniffed, smiled and turned her back to me. I definitely glanced at that fat ass. I couldn't help it; she had the body of a goddess and her swag was amazing to me. I loved a female that knew how to dress. She also had her own shit and back in the day, she was known for being one of the baddest bitches in Memphis.

"I'll go get, Kalissa, you stay right here." She closed the door behind her, but not all the way.

I watched that ass until it disappeared. I didn't start feeling guilty until she was gone away from me for about a full minute. Then I pounded my hand against my head. "Stupid, stupid, stupid."

Bubbie appeared in the doorway. "JaMichael, what are you doing here? It's only been ten days; not even a month yet."

I took ahold of her and kissed her soft lips. I hugged her and sniffed her. She felt and smelled so good, though I could tell she didn't have on any perfume. "Baby, before you curse me out, here." I grabbed the Zale's box out of the Louis bag and handed it to her.

"What is this?" I didn't give a fuck how mad Bubbie had ever been at me, she always took her gifts. She opened the box and saw the lemonade colored, female Rolex flooded in ice. "Dang, boy, where you get this from?"

"This go wit' it, lil' mama and this one." I handed her two more boxes.

She sat on her mother's porch and opened each one, revealing the two-carat lemonade earrings and the matching bracelet. I'd dropped a quick hundred and twenty-five thousand and didn't even care. I loved Bubbie and the longer I stayed away from her the more I was starting to see that. "Baybeeee, what are you doing?"

I squatted beside her, peeped her mother standing in the doorway trying to be as inconspicuous as she possibly could and didn't even care. "Bubbie, I love you, baby! I love you and I love our boys. I wanna do right by you. I mean I know I'm not perfect, but I love you so much baby. I don't want to lose you ever."

She covered her mouth with her hand. She had already placed the Rolex on her right wrist as it sparkled in the night just from the few lights her mother had on the porch of her mansion. "Don't say that. It's only been ten days. What has changed so drastically in ten days?"

I took hold of her shoulders. "Being away from you. I can't Lil' mama, I need yo' lil' butt, seriously." I pulled her to a standing position.

She looked into my eyes with her almond-shaped ones. Her mouth remained open, I could see her tooth that was just in the back of her lower row of teeth. The small imperfection made her look that much sexier to me. For some reason, I was yearning for her in a way I had never yearned for her before.

"Honey, are you saying you are sure all that old stuff is out of your system?"

"Look, baby, I don't know, but what I do know is that I love you. I'm willing to try and conquer myself every second of every day if it means, I'll have you. I miss you, boo. I'll change for you, that's on my word."

"Uh-huh." She covered her mouth again.

"So, what do you say, Bubbie?" I was thirsty. I needed her back in my arms tonight.

Her mother opened the door further and I saw the two of them make eye contact. Then Bubbie frowned and faced me. "I can't do that, right now, JaMichael. My father said all these same things to my mother when he was at his lowest points. He never changed and he tried and tried. You've only been trying for ten days. There is no way you've changed already."

"Yes, I have, damn!" I mugged Yvonne. "Yo' pops ain't got nothin' to do wit' me. It ain't our bidness how he treated your mother, fuck dude."

"JaMichael!" Bubbie gasped.

"I care about you, I'm trying to make this right with you. Please, lil' mama, at least let me see the twins."

"JaMichael, you can see your sons at any time. I ain't holding them away from you, I would never do that."

"Good, cause I wanna see them, right now." I made my way toward the front door.

Bubbie grabbed my wrist. "Wait, are you serious about changing for me and missing me like crazy?"

"Yes, lil' mama, please come back to Daddy. Let me hold you down." I pulled her into my arms and kissed her neck. She had small freckles all over it, it made her look so sexy.

She hugged me tight. "I missed you too, Daddy. I swear I been thinking about you every second of every day. All I want is for us to have a happy home. I need us to have a strong family. It all starts with the man."

"Okay, baby, that's cool. Just let me hold you for a minute." I held her tight and inhaled her natural scent.

"JaMichael, why don't you start by coming to Kingdom Hall with us this Sunday," Yvonne offered.

I looked up at her. "What?"

"Church baby, I think you and Kalissa would have a stronger connection if Jehovah was in the middle of you two. So, how about it?" Yvonne asked, hopeful.

"Yeah, Daddy, how about it? We could have a nice lunch afterward, maybe even a picnic with just you and I. Mama wouldn't mind watching the kids would you mama?"

Yvonne shook her head. "Sho' wouldn't."

"So, whatta you say?"

Jahliya pulled up the long driveway and parked before jumping out of her Benz. "JaMichael, you gotta get to the hospital."

I released Bubbie and made my way over to her worried. "Why, what's good?" I didn't know what was going on.

"Tamia been in labor for twelve hours, she finna have the baby."

I cringed, by the time I looked over my, shoulder Bubbie was already being led into the house with Yvonne's arm around her neck. "Baby! Baby!" I started walking toward them.

Bubbie started closing the door. "Just go to her, JaMichael, go to your other family." She broke into tears before she closed the door.

Ghost

Chapter 12

Two days later, I sat holding my son, Damien in my arms. I couldn't believe how much he looked like my twins, Ja-Michael and KaMichael. His dimples were as deep as mine and theirs. I felt blessed that another healthy child had been born into this world to me. I had done a lot of wrongs, I was just thankful that, this far, God hadn't cast down the fires of punishment unto my children. I was a strong believer in karma and every second of every day my payback from the universe and when it would take place for the wrongs that I had done was in the back of my mind.

Tamia leaned over my lap and stroked Damien's arm. She smiled at me and laid her head on my shoulder. "It's crazy how much this lil' boy look just like your Father, JaMichael. I'm surprised you didn't name him after him," she said, stroking the side of his cheek.

I looked down at him. "I thought about it, but my pops got a lot of sins already on him. I don't wanna project none of that onto our son. He needs a fresh start." I kissed his cheek.

She nodded. "Yeah, I guess, you're right. But how about this, you gave him his first name, which is Damien right?"

"Right, I'm still trying to get a feel for him before we put it on his birth certificate, but yeah, that's the name I'm leaning toward."

"Okay, then why don't we at least give him your father's middle name. He can be called, Damien Taurus Stevens, in honor of your Pops."

I held him more in my arms, Damien opened his eyes and squinted. Then he closed them again and yawned. His little fingers flexed and balled into a fist. I smiled, damn, he had some real deep dimples. He did look just like my Pops, though. "You know what, them people finna kill my father anyway, right?"

Tamia nodded in silence. "Yeah, they are."

"And I am his only son, right?"

She nodded again and kissed our son on the cheek. "That's right, baby."

I took a deep breath and looked back at my child again. "A'ight den, it's settled. His name in honor of my Pops, who never had a chance in life, is going to be Taurus Damien Stevens." I held him up in my arms. "How do you like the sound of that, Taurus, huh?"

He frowned and yawned again, then opened his eyes, flashing his baby blues, and started crying. I cuffed him back to my chest and kissed him on the top of his curly head. There was a knock at the door.

Jahliya stuck her head inside of the room, then came all the way inside. "Hey, y'all." She had a bottle of Moët in her right hand and a single red rose for Tamia in her left. "Congratulations." She handed me the bottle and slipped Taurus in her arms, and gave Tamia the red rose, after kissing her on the cheek.

"Taurus Damien Stevens." Tamia smiled.

"What?" Jahliya asked.

"That's his name, we just decided on it. It's Taurus Damien Stevens, in honor of your father." Tamia snuggled up closer to me.

Jahliya held him in the air and looked him over. She turned her head sideways and nodded. "Yeah, he do look just like, Daddy, that's crazy." She hugged him to her chest and sat on the couch with him.

I started to get up when Tamia grabbed my arm and pulled me back so that I sat on the side of her. "JaMichael, we need to talk for a minute." She took one of the juices from her trays and sipped out of it. Though there were slight bags under her eyes from the physical exertion of labor, she still looked beautiful.

I was having a hard time looking at her because it was bringing back old thoughts, feelings, and emotions from when we were younger. "What's good, Tamia?" I was checking my phone to make sure Bubbie hadn't hit me up and she hadn't. I felt sick about that fact.

Tamia adjusted herself on her pillow. "Well, I guess, I just need to know what it's finna be. You finna stand up and be with me? Or are you finna keep running the streets and leave me to fend for myself raising our son, who is going to need your presence every step of the way?"

"Tamia, I ain't got time for these questions, right now, Shawty. I got a plate full of shit I gotta be doing."

"That's fine, but now that he is here, he needs to be at the top of your list every time. I am not going to be able to raise him on my own and I shouldn't have, too. You're supposed to be there."

"Whoa, whoa, whoa! Man stop playin' wit' me. You should already know, I'ma stand up as a man and handle my bidness. For as long as I got air in my lungs you, nor him ain't gone have to need for shit. I'ma make sure I pay all your bills and keep you beyond straight. In fact, as soon as you step out of this hospital, I'ma cash you out wit' a bag, know that." I stood up, dusted off my clothes and adjusted my black iced Rolex.

"Why are you trying to come at me as if I'm some sort of groupie? I ain't money hungry and I ain't all thirsty to be with yo' ass. I still love you and I guess a major part of me just wanna know what happened to us?"

I shrugged my shoulders. "I don't know, you started messing with Chino, I guess once that came out, I started looking at you different. You lied to me and you betrayed me by going behind my back."

She gasped. "JaMichael, are you kidding me, right now? You just had two twins by a female who has been my only enemy since I was in the fuckin' fourth grade. You was fuckin' her behind my back. So, please tell me who betrayed who?"

I ain't have no comeback for that because she basically busted my head with that one. Instead of admitting she had a point I took the low road. "So, what you told me, Chino was your cousin. When all along that nigga was your pimp. You probably was fuckin' him the whole time you and I were together. Come to think of it, every time he came through Memphis you rolled off with him for a few hours. As good as yo' pussy is, he was probably able to get right a few times."

She shook her head. "I never fucked him, until I found out you was fuckin' wit', Kalissa. You took my virginity and you know you did. But if your only defense for not wanting to be with me now is because of a mistake, I made with him, then cool. I'll just woman up and take care of my bidness like a true Queen. I got this." She adjusted her pillow again before laying back on it and pulled the sheet up.

Something musta took place under it, because she threw it off and felt her breasts. "Jahliya, let me see him my chest's leaking again.

Jahliya stood up with Taurus in her arms and handed him to Tamia, after kissing his cheeks. She took hold of my arm and pulled me into the bathroom. "We'll be right back lil' sis."

I came in and mugged her lil' ass. "Why the fuck you grabbing me all rough and shit?"

She closed the bathroom door and locked it. Then turned on the sink as high as it could go. She pointed at me. "Nigga, I'll buss you in yo' shit. What the fuck is wrong with you?"

"What is you talking about?"

"You standing out there acting like some dead beat ass baller. Thinking you can throw that drug money in these lil' girl's faces and that's going to be enough to string them along. JaMichael, you look real trifling, I swear to God it's making me wanna kick yo' ass."

"What the fuck else am I supposed to do?"

Smack!

Jahliya hit me hard, then she grabbed me by the shirt, and pointed in my face. "Lil' nigga watch yo' mouth when you talk to me. I am your big sister and the only mother you got. You not finna address me like you be addressing these lil' girls and think it's sweet." She released me and pushed me back.

I loved my sister, I swear to God there was nobody else in the world that could've got away with what she was doing to me at that moment. Anybody else and I would of either beat them senseless or blew their head off their neck. "A'ight, sis, I apologize." I hated it when Jahliya was mad at me. Out of all the people in the world, I hated failing her the most.

"You ain't got no reason to apologize to me. You need to be out there conducting yourself as a man and apologizing to both of your children's mothers. Think about how you would do another nigga if you found out he was treating me like you're treating them. JaMichael, you would lose it. That fuck nigga would be dead in a matter of seconds, as soon as you found out."

I sighed and lowered my head. "Damn, Jahliya, you always on my ass sis. You need to tell me what I should do? I got two females, both that I care about in their own way. They got my babies and they both wanna be with me. Somebody gotta get the short end of the stick."

"And I'm telling you, right now, that when it comes down to situations like these, it's always the children that wind up getting the short end, always. You need to find a way to make it work for all three of y'all."

"How do I do that?" I felt so damn lost and irritated. It seemed like pussy was always getting me in trouble.

"You need to go out there and tuck your tail. Tell that girl some shit that's going to feed her emotions. She just had your baby. She's feeling used, lost, abandoned and probably like her life is over. She is extremely prone to postpartum depression, which could be dangerous for her and Taurus. You don't want these girls resenting your children. Trust me on this lil', bruh. Get yo' ass out there and make it happen and remember, it's not about you."

***

When I got out of the bathroom, Tamia was wiping her eyes with a Kleenex, while Taurus nursed at her. She held him in her left arm. I came and sat on the side of the bed. She looked up at me and sniffled.

"Tamia, I'm sorry for how I been treating you, and how I been acting. I just wanna let you know, I appreciate you for carrying my son and giving him life. I owe you more than I could ever repay you."

She nodded. "Thank you for saying that. I definitely needed to hear it." She broke into a fit of tears. "I'm so stupid, I knew you wasn't going to be with me and this child. I should've got rid of him back when I still could." She started breaking down so much that Taurus took his mouth off her nipple and started wailing at the top of his lungs.

Jahliya slipped on the side of me and took him away. "Y'all fix this."

I slid beside Tamia, wrapped my arm around her neck and pulled her to my chest. "Tamia's please, don't cry, Shawty. I said I was sorry."

"But why don't you care about me, JaMichael? Why do you hate me so much? I've never meant to hurt you. I still love you with all my heart, now I don't even know if I want this baby if you ain't part of our lives, I had him for you." She cried harder.

Damn, I was feeling like shit. I was too young to be going through this shit, but then again, I guess both Bubbie and Tamia could be saying the same thing, not to mention, I couldn't forget about Danyelle, that situation was still open and I needed to find a solution to it. I felt trapped on so many levels. "Tamia, Tamia, baby, listen me."

"*Baby*, why the fuck are you calling her baby?" Bubbie said, stepping all the way into the hospital room.

Tamia had been crying so loudly that I had not been able to hear her. I perked up.

Tamia wiped her tears and looked over at Bubbie who was taking her spring Chanel leather off, placing it on the arm of the couch. "Bubbie, what the fuck are you doing in my room?"

"Bitch what the fuck are you doing crying all in my man's arms? He ain't finna fall for that shit."

"Ain't nobody trying to make him fall for nothing. Get out of my room," Tamia returned, sniffling.

"Ain't." Bubbie rushed around the bed. She had a scowl on her face. "And you sitting in this fuckin' room calling this bitch, baby? What is wrong with you? I'm the only baby, you got." She swung.

I blocked that shit and scooped her lil' ass up, taking her into the bathroom. I passed Jahliya who was shaking her head and bouncing Taurus up and down on her knee. When we made it inside of the bathroom, Bubbie turned to me and pushed me hard as she could.

"Why the fuck you calling her, baby? You think you finna leave me for her? Me and your twins? Nigga, on my life, I will kill you and that caramel bitch." She swung again.

I ducked and grabbed her arms pinning her against the wall. "Shawty, I love yo' crazy ass, but if you swing and one of those blows connect, I'm fuckin' you up and I ain't gon' feel no type of way about it cause I done told you about putting your hands on me."

She yanked her arms free. "Nigga, fuck you, answer my question. Why are you calling that bitch, baby?"

Tamia beat on the door. "Open the door, JaMichael, I'll tell her punk ass why you called me that."

"Oh, really move, JaMichael. I'm finna beat this bitch ass once and for all." Bubbie grabbed the knob and pulled the door open, with strength I didn't even know she possessed.

Chapter 13

She rushed into the hospital room and Tamia threw up her guards. Her breasts were lactating. There were two wet circles surrounding her nipples. Yet, instead, she paid no attention to that. Her focus was on getting into Bubbie's ass. "Let's go."

Bubbie tried her best to fight around but I wasn't moving. "Move, JaMichael, she acting all tough, let me get her." She jumped and reached for Tamia again.

Taurus was hollering at the top of his lungs and I saw that Jahliya was looking for somewhere to put him. The room was full of chaos and confusion. I pulled Bubbie all the way back toward the bathroom, I actually picked her up. Tamia ran over and reached across my back to slap her. She got her good, too. Now Bubbie was kicking her legs widely. She was trying to break free by any means. When Tamia jumped on my back and slapped her again, I knew I had to let her go, so I did.

Bubbie rushed her like a pure, cold-blooded animal. She grabbed Tamia with two hands around the neck and slammed her into the wall. She picked her up and flung her to the floor. She got on top of her and started fucking her up. Tamia could-n't do nothing but accept the ass-whoopin' Bubbie was giving her. I think it was because she was still weak from having Taurus that Bubbie was able to take her so easily. I'd seen Tamia fight on more than a few occasions, she was a beast, but this day she was not.

By the time, I pulled a kicking and scratching Bubbie off her she was bleeding from the mouth and had scratches all over her face. I was pissed at the both of them, equally.

"That's all right, Bubbie, bitch you won this round. You got me. You caught me while I was all weak and shit. A'ight, just remember this shit ain't over, it ain't over by a long shot."

She wiped her mouth and saw that it was blood on the back of her hand.

"Bitch you asked for it, you should've never slapped me in my face. I don't give a fuck you just havin' a kid. I had two! And what?"

Tamia nodded and laughed sinisterly. "I got you, I got both of y'all. Watch." She looked at her bloody hand again, after touching her nose and lip. "Get the fuck out of my room, both of y'all! Get the fuck out of my room, right now. Security! Security! Help!" she hollered.

Jahliya ran up behind her and covered her mouth with her hand. "Sis, stop that rat shit. That ain't in you or none of us."

Tamia moved her hand on top of Jahliya's as if she was going to fight her to get her hand from over her mouth, but then she musta decided against it. She simply stood there and huffed and puffed, eyeing both me and Bubbie.

"Y'all finna sit y'all asses down and both of you are going to listen to what the fuck I gotta say. Sit down, Bubbie!"

Bubbie took a seat on the couch with no problem. She crossed her thick thighs and took one of the juices from Tamia's tray and opened it, downing the contents. She burped and dropped the empty container on the floor, on her petty shit.

Tamia growled and stomped her right foot.

Jahliya leaned into her ear. "Tamia, when I let you go you need to go sit on your bed and chill. Both of y'all need to hear me out. Nod your head if you understand."

Tamia nodded.

Jahliya let her go. "JaMichael, you go sit on the couch, too.

I did.

"Bitch don't leave your trash in my room neither. I know yo' mama was too busy in the streets to teach you any home training, but that ain't got shit to do with me," Tamia snapped, at Bubbie.

Bubbie kicked the juice container across the floor and crossed her arms. "You pick that shit up. You should be used to trash being all on the floor where you lay yo' head anyway, wit' yo' broke ass."

Tamia smacked her lips and waved her off. "Bitch whatever.

***

Jahliya paced for a second, then she stopped. She shook her head. Both Tamia and Bubbie's eyes were glued on her, as well as my own. "Look, I love my brother. He means the world to me, but I gotta be honest you two are tripping." She ran her fingers through her curly hair. "Ain't no man worthy enough to make two beautiful women, such as yourselves, be fighting over him like this. If anything, he should be fighting, and ready to kill over you two. You have given him precious children. Angels, gifts, that he will never be able to return to you. For that very reason alone, he owes both of you the world."

Bubbie looked at Tamia and both women rolled their eyes at the other at the same damn time. It was almost comical. "Both of you are mothers now. You don't have time to be fighting each other or fighting to kill one another. Your first priority should be those children. Women that fight over men look so stupid, especially if he ain't worth it and as much as I love my brother, he ain't did nothing for either one of you to show you he deserves the fight from either of you. Y'all in a perfect world should be coming together to whoop his ass."

"Hey," I interrupted, mugging the shit out of Jahliya. "Where are you going with this?"

"They should be asking you that same question about their children's futures, as well as their own. They are fighting the wrong person, JaMichael, and you know they are."

"Man, I ain't telling them to fight over me. That shit seems childish as hell."

"Yeah, but you ain't doing nothing to stop us from fighting over you either," Bubbie said, standing up. "Look, you're right, Jahliya. We should value ourselves more than this. There is no reason why a beautiful woman and a less cute woman, should be fighting over a man." She looked over at Tamia and smirked. "So, this is how this is finna go down. JaMichael, you need to make a choice, right here, right now. Which one of us are you going to be with?"

I stood up and laughed. "Y'all tripping like a ma'fucka. Look, I'm choosing my kids, that's who I'm choosing. It's too much shit going on in my life for me to sit here and decide who I'm finna try and be with."

"You can't just choose the kids, JaMichael. That's your way of being able to bounce back and forth from household to household. You need to make a decision?"

"You know what, no he don't. I'm not finna sit around and wait for some indecisive man to choose me. I'm gon' make the decision for him because I don't want his ass no more. I choose myself. I am woman enough to do this on my own if I have, too. She needs him more than I do," Tamia said, getting up, opening the door to her hospital room. "Now, I need all of you to leave, so my baby can get some sleep."

Bubbie stood up. "Wait a minute bitch, why you have to say all that? Why you just couldn't say you're good and keep it moving. That's always been your problem. You love bumping yo' gums a lil' bit too much."

"Bitch, I said what I said, now bye," Tamia returned.

Jahliya rubbed her temples. "You lil' girls is getting on my nerves. Y'all ain't listen to nothing I just said."

"That's her, she always gotta have the last word," Bubbie accused, nodding her head at Tamia.

"Y'all gotta get the fuck out of my room, seriously. I'm getting a headache. Leave!" Tamia demanded.

"Don't be hollering at nobody," Bubbie snapped.

"Yeah, girl you being rude as hell. Let me kiss my nephew before I go." Jahliya made her way over to Taurus.

Tamia rushed over and picked him up. "Nope, you had enough kisses for one day. Go to this bitch house and kiss all over them ugly babies she just had."

"*Ugly*? Aw, you really got me fucked up now." Bubbie tried to make it to her with rage steaming out of her.

I picked her up. "Come on, man. Let's just get out of here."

"Why I can't kiss my nephew, Tamia? Now you just being petty." Jahliya asked looking like she was heated.

"Because I said so, bye, Jahliya." Tamia held Taurus in her arms and bounced him up and down.

Jahliya walked past her and nodded her head. "It's all good, I hope you feel better, Tamia and I love you Taurus." She waved bye to him and mugged Tamia before stepping into the hallway.

I set Bubbie down and nudged her to follow Jahliya. She acted as if she didn't want to at first, but then she reluctantly went with her stride for stride. I turned to Tamia. "Look, ma, I'ma be there for my son. You definitely ain't gotta worry about doing this on your own. I got your back, I've always had it."

"The police been sweating me about Chino's murder. Before I went into labor, they came and hollered at me three times. I didn't tell them shit. I can't believe you gon' do me like this," Tamia said, holding the back of Taurus's head.

I stood there looking at her for a full thirty seconds, before I responded, "Why would you all of a sudden say some shit like that?"

"Gone with that bitch, JaMichael. I don't need you, Taurus don't need you either. Just remember that hell hath no fury like a woman scorned." She blinked tears.

I stepped closer. "What you saying, you finna tell Twelve what happened or some shit?" I felt myself becoming irate.

"Bye, JaMichael, I hope you live your best life." She tried to slam the door.

I put my foot in the crack, stopping her from doing so. I forced the door open and stepped into her room. "You finna tell the law what happened with dude, huh? That'll be stupid, because they gon' ask about that lil' bitch, too. Then what?"

"Get out of my room, JaMichael, kick rocks." She pushed me and slammed the door. "I hate you!" she screamed.

***

Later that night, Bubbie slid into the passenger's seat of my red Porsche and closed the door. I was parked in front of her mother's mansion trying to get a piece of mind. I was still reeling off what had taken place with Tamia. I didn't know if she was saying, she was about to go to the authorities and tell them what happened the night I rescued her from Chino. Or if she was just throwing that hint out there to scare me. Either way, I was thinking about whacking her ass. I was literally about ninety-five percent sure, I was going to have too, and that fact was crushing my soul. So, when Bubbie slid into the passenger's seat I was in another world.

She nudged me. "What you thinking about, JaMichael? Don't lie either."

I came out of my zone and looked out the front window. It was beginning to drizzle. "Tamia."

"Uh—damn, you ain't have to be that honest. What you thinking about her for?"

"Nall, it ain't like that, she just said some real foul shit to me before I left the hospital. I been replaying it in my head ever since. I'm trying to figure out what I'm finna do."

"I know you ain't talking about when she said, she chooses herself? What now since she said that it's making you want her or something? Ugh, that's what I'm saying, that bitch always had a stronghold on you. She ain't mean that shit. I hope you ain't feeling sorry for her when we got two kids in the house. Two that I would never keep from you or Jahliya. You just need to—"

"Bubbie! Shut the fuck up," I snapped.

She tensed and bucked her eyes at me. Then hunched over and exhaled. "What's going on, JaMichael?"

"You just be running your mouth too much. Shut the fuck up and let me think."

She opened the passenger's door and stepped outside. "Fuck you, JaMichael. You love that bitch that much, then you can raise them twins on your own." She slammed the door and took off running down the driveway, just as it was beginning to storm hard.

"Fuck." Lightning flashed across the sky and thunder roared loudly. The next thing I knew the rain was coming down so hard that it sounded like rice hitting the top of my Porsche.

Bubbie tripped and fell face-first to the ground. She sat down, crossed her arms around her knees and rocked back and forth. Then she got up and took off running again just as a lightning bolt struck a tree not more than twenty feet away from her. She fell again and this time laid there.

I shot out of my Porsche and ran down the long driveway, into the brush of woods. When I got to her side, I could hear her crying loudly. I kneeled down and picked her up. "Baby, what the fuck are you doing?"

"You wanna be with her, JaMichael. You don't want me. I don't know what it is about me, but you are choosing her. I'ma kill that, bitch," she cried.

"Bubbie, you're bugging Shawty. I don't want her, I need you baby. You're the only woman I need. Now stop acting so fuckin' crazy."

She smacked my arms away. "Get off me!" She stood up. "*Crazy—crazy*, how the fuck you gon' call me crazy when you're the one driving me to insanity? I got yo' two kids, I been fighting for you since high school, even with people trying to kill both of our assess. Now you sitting out here parked in front of my mother's mansion, thinking about some other bitch. But you got the audacity to call me crazy, I can't handle this." She took off running.

The rain was coming down so hard my thin T-shirt and shorts felt like leather on my skin. It thundered loudly as lightning flashed across the sky. On top of that, it was getting very windy so much so, I was having a hard time staying on my two feet.

Bubbie ran sideways almost. She fought to keep moving forward. The wind seemed to get stronger and stronger. "I can't take this no more," she said over and over. She ran for about fifty yards, the wind knocked her over and made her roll on the ground. She struggled to get to her feet.

I fought against the elements and ran as fast as I could to get to her. I fell more than once. The wind was doing its best to prevent me from getting to her. It whistled, then howled loudly. Rain splashed into my face harshly, I wiped it away and kept running. By the time, I made it to Bubbie she was almost off her feet. The wind was pulling her back. About a hundred yards from her a big tornado funnel had formed. It caused the trees to move violently. The rain became a weapon against both of us.

Bubbie reached out to me. "JaMichael, help me, please!" She screamed and reached for me.

The wind became so harsh, I felt like I was being pushed back. I fought forward as hard as I could. Our fingers touched but then she was sucked away from me again. I lowered my head and felt the rain slapping me. It felt like hail. I kept my eyes open as far as I could, but even then, they were lower than slits. I reached as far as I could, wiggling my fingers.

"JaMichael, please help me!"

I jerked forward and tangled fingers with Bubbie. As soon as they interlocked, I pulled and grabbed her wrists and yanked her to me. She crashed into my chest and my arms went around her body. I fell to the ground with her. The pulling from the Tornado became intense. It sounded like the loudest piercing scream I had ever heard in my entire life and it felt like it lasted for a full hour, but lucky for us, it only lasted a few minutes. Then it was going on its way in the opposite direction of us. The pulling lessened and after a few seconds, we were left with rain and a strong thunderstorm.

Ghost

Chapter 14

Bubbie took off her wet top and slung it to the floor. She kicked her door closed, and locked it, before reaching behind her back, unhooking her bra. When her titties fell out my dick got hard as a rock. I had never seen them so full before and I had watched her feed my sons on more than one occasion. She eyed me and looked hungry.

I slid my wet Polo shirt over my head and dropped it to the floor, then pulled off my black tank top. "What's wrong with you, lil' mama?"

She kept making her way over to me. "I want some of my daddy right here, right now." She kissed my lips and pushed me into the wall aggressive as hell.

I gripped her fat ass booty and sucked her neck. I could taste her perfume, mixed with the rain. She smelled so good, I was fiending for some of that pussy. Ever since our lil' ones had arrived she hadn't given me any. I squeezed that ass like it was my first time squeezing it. It felt soft, yet, firm. The closer my fingers got to her crack, the hotter it got. I picked her up, tossed her on the bed, unbuckled her belt and pulled her pants down and off throwing them against the wall. I ripped her panties off and kneeled with my face between her thighs, licking up and down her slit. I didn't know if it was from the rain or from her excitement, either way, my tongue was all up in her, hungrily.

"Uh! Uh! Yes, Daddy, I need you." She opened her thighs further, forcing me deeper into her center. She raised her ass from the bed and rode my face.

I slurped, licked, then slurped and licked some more. My tongue shot in and out of her box before I slipped two fingers inside of her. I scooted all the way up on the bed and picked her ass up. She grabbed the headboard and straddled my face cowgirl, riding it swiftly.

"Yes! Yes, Daddy, aw shit. Uhhhh, fuck—yes!" The headboard clapped into the wall over and over, she was so wet it felt like she was peeing in my mouth.

I located her clit and sucked hard, running back and forth across it with my tongue. Every time I hit her button she jerked and became wetter.

She took four deep breaths and came all over me. "Oh-oh, Daddyyy!" She held on to the headboard for support, while she went through the motions of an explosive orgasm.

I kept right on licking and sucking until she climbed off me. My tongue traced my lips, I could still taste her. That fact alone had me geeked.

"Lay down." she ordered. As soon as I did, she unzipped my pants and pulled out my dick. She stroked it up and down and kissed all over it. "This my dick, you belong to me. I love you more than any other bitch ever could." She sucked me into her mouth and came on to her knees.

Her fat ass booty was in the air, I wasted no time rubbing it. My hand snuck into her crease. I felt the slippery lips and slipped two fingers back into her, pulled them out and sucked them into my mouth. She tasted salty and so good to me. I loved the taste of my baby mother's pussy.

She bobbed her head into my lap faster and faster, then popped me out. "Cum for me, Daddy. Cum for me!" Then she was sucking again.

My toes curled, I humped up from the bed and started stroking her mouth. She nipped at my head with her teeth and twirled her tongue around it over and over again. When her digit, licked my pee hole, I shuddered and came in spurts. She pulled me out and pumped her fist, milking me. Cum shot into the air and around her fist before she sucked me back in and swallowed everything I had to offer. I continued to shudder that shit felt so good. She popped me back out and cleaned up the loose cum all over my lower region.

"That's what you get, Daddy. I'm finna lock yo' ass down. You supposed to be with me." She slid two fingers into her pussy and worked them in and out, before straddling me, and taking hold of my hard piece, sliding down on it. "Oooo," she moaned.

My eyes were on those sexy titties, the nipples leaked milk, while she rode me. It dribbled out of the small holes inside of her nipples, then onto her stomach and my chest. It felt hot, and oh so good. I leaned my head forwards and pinched them.

"Uhhhh!" Milk squirted out, she rode me faster. "Stop, Daddy, please stop!"

I brought her closer to me, trapped a nipple in my mouth and sucked hard. While I grabbed her waist and made her fuck me faster. "Ride me, Bubbie! Ride Daddy, baby!" I went right back to sucking.

"Mmm-mmm-mmm, okay! Yes, mmm, shit—shit, Daddy!" She slapped her middle against mine making sure she stayed low enough to keep her nipple in my mouth.

I kept on switching back and forth from one nipple to the other. The taste of her milk was driving me crazy. I knew I had helped create it and that it was because of her that my children had life. The liquid became sacred, yet, erotic to me. I needed more and more of it. I flipped her on all fours and beat that pussy hard while her new sized titties rubbed up and down the sheets leaking all over them. Her nipples stood out about an inch from her areoles. It looked so sexy with her thick ass cheeks getting beat in. Bubbie had become super strapped. Thick, and well put together and I was loving every inch of that womb.

I couldn't believe how tight and snug her cat felt around me. "Uh, this my pussy! This my pussy, shit, this my pussy!" I hollered dicking her ass down.

She came, hollering at the top of her lungs and fell on her stomach with me hammering away from the back. I kept plunging and plunging. That pussy kept getting better and better. She screamed for the fifth time and I came deep within her womb, pumping my seed. I stayed planted deep, jerking and sucking on the back of her neck.

When I finally pulled out, I licked down her spine and bit on her skin softly, until I got to her booty cheeks. "I love you, boo."

She moaned, "Baby, girl loves you too, Daddy."

I opened them cheeks and kissed her right on the sweaty rosebud, delved my tongue inside of her and ran it in and out, while my thumb went from side to side on her clitoris. Then I sucked her thick ass cheeks while she played with her clit and kept coming back to back. I musta fingered that ass for a half hour and tasted her treasures back there. She was screaming so loud her mother started beating on the door.

**

Bubbie woke me up at three in the morning by straddling me. She kissed my lips, I could feel her hot pussy on my waist. "Daddy—Dadddyyy, wake up." She licked my lips.

I slowly opened my eyes, when they came into focus, I saw that it was still lightning outside. The rain was a steady pitter-patter on her windowpane. "What's good, baby? Damn, I'm sleeping."

"Your phone been ringing off the hook for an hour straight. I was gon' answer it, but I didn't feel like hearing your mouth." She touched my lips with her finger. It still smelled like pussy, I liked that.

"Why you ain't wake me up a whole ass hour ago then?"

"Cause, I was too sleepy. Besides, I figured it wasn't nothing but one of them lil' thots out there. I ain't finna be waking up my man for them they'll be okay," she grunted and rolled her eyes.

"Hand me my phone, Lil' Mama."

She slid off me and walked over to the dresser with her ass cheeks jiggling out of control. She was caramel but the closer you got to the bottom of her ass cheeks, the darker they became. I found that part of her imperfectly perfect. She grabbed the phone and came back. Her pussy lips smushed into each other before she climbed on to the bed.

Bubbie was bad, I was starting to realize that all over again. "Here."

I grabbed the phone and the first thing I read across the screen was that the wrong pin number had been entered five times. I looked over at Bubbie and she looked off. I shook my head and entered the right one. A text message came across the screen from Nikki, Shemar and Phoenix.

Nikki: Hey JaMichael, I need to get up with you immediately. Get back to me asap.

Shemar: Hey bruh, hit me back asap!

Phoenix: Get at me asap! It's urgent!

I sat up in bed. "Look, I gotta go, Lil' Mama."

"Really, who is it? Is it that bitch, Tamia?"

"N'all, it's Nikki, Shemar, and Phoenix. Something must've jumped off and I gotta get ahead of it once I find out what it is. You already know how this Cartel shit work."

"Yeah, I guess," she said low.

I jumped up naked. "Damn, where my clothes?"

She slid to the foot of the bed and stood up. "I gotta put them in the dryer, I'll be right back." Before I could say anything, she rushed out of the room.

I stayed there looking at my phone. I wanted to call one of the three people that had gotten in touch with me, but I already knew the news couldn't be good. So, even though curiosity was going to kill me until I found out what was going on, I was going to wait. I musta been looking down at my phone for every bit of two minutes when something told me to look up. When I did, I was shocked to find Yvonne in the doorway, watching me. Her eyes traveled up and down my body. She didn't know that I was watching her until she bit into her bottom lip and trailed her eyes up into mine.

Then she jerked back as if caught off guard. "JaMichael, uh, I was just finna make sure you and Kalissa was okay. Y'all don't need nothing do you?"

I shook my head. "Nall, we good."

Her eyes trialed back down to my dick and it began to swell up all on its own. All because this vet was looking at my piece and how it hung low. "Okay, baby, well that's good to know. Y'all ain't arguing no more are you?"

'*Really*?' I thought. This was the best she could come up with to make conversation. "Nall, we good, Yvonne, but thank you for asking."

She nodded. "Okay, baby, have a good night." Before she left, I noticed that both of her nipples were rock hard through her blouse.

Bubbie stepped into the room and saw me standing there naked. "I know my mother wasn't just in here while you were standing like that, was she?" She looked over her shoulder back out of the door.

I laughed. "Yeah, she saw what ya baby daddy was working wit' and she looked thirsty, too. You better be careful, or else I'ma be all up in ya moms."

Bubbie frowned and pushed me. "Don't play wit' me like that, JaMichael. I can already tell my mama likes yo' stupid ass and I don't know how much. She real vulnerable right now, so don't even play wit' me like that."

I nodded. "Baby, I'm sorry, I didn't mean nothing by it. I got you, though. You sure that's the only thing that's the matter?"

She walked away from me and sat on the bed. "JaMichael, are we going to be together or not?"

I stepped in front of her. "Yeah, boo, I'ma settle down and hold you down like I'm supposed to. I don't give a fuck about none of those other hoes out there. I just wanna make you happy."

"JaMichael, you saying that shit now, but as soon as you run across one of those bad bitches out there, you gon' be trying to smash. Now you already know how you are. I'ma ask you again. Are you and I going to be together or do you still need room to mature? I need to know if you're going to be with me faithfully?"

My phone started buzzing like crazy and I was glad. Bubbie had me up against the ropes, I didn't know what to say at that moment. So, I used my phone as a reason to say nothin' at all.

Ghost

Chapter 15

Nikki met me at the airport in Houston the next morning. When I jumped into her Bentley, she looked sick on the stomach. It was nice and bright outside. It felt like it was every bit of eighty degrees, with a light breeze. I opened the passenger's door, slid into the seat and it struck me as odd when she didn't say a word.

I tossed my bag on the backseat. "What's good, Nikki? Why you so quiet?"

She looked over her shoulder and backed the Bentley out of the parking space, before putting it in drive, stepping on the gas. "Some fucked up shit happened, JaMichael."

She had my full attention. "What?"

"You remember Shemar had his daughter Nicole and his baby mother Syndie come over here in Texas, right?"

"Yeah, I met his daughter a few nights ago. She straight?" I started imagining how cold her body was and my brain took on a life of its own.

"Yeah, well since she was down in Houston, Syndie must've figured she'd invite some of her other family over for a cookout with Shemar's people, seeing as they were only over in Fort Worth. All I can say is, well the Sinaloa ma'fuckas ain't no joke. They showed up and did the damn thang."

My eyes bugged out of my head. "They got a hold of his people?"

She sighed and nodded. "Yeah and Shemar all fucked up about it. You already know how we get down so it ain't like we can go to the police. We just gotta take this shit on the chin and find a way to get even." She rolled on the highway and switched lanes twice until she was in the speeding lane. Once there, she stepped on the gas and pushed her Bentley to the limit.

I was speechless, I didn't know what to say, or even think. I was simply imagining what would happen if the Sinaloas attacked those that I loved? What would I do? I wondered if I would be able to keep it together?

Nikki reached over and grabbed my hand. She placed hers on top of mine and laced her fingers with my own. The feeling was weird. A little more intimate than I was used to coming from her, but it also told me she was hurting, and this was her way of feeling closer to me in a time when she needed somebody. I was already preparing for an extremely broken Shemar.

"I'm glad you came, JaMichael. I don't mean to be on that sappy shit, but I missed yo' fine ass. There is something about your presence that calms my soul." She kissed my cheek and kept on rolling.

I eyed her thick thighs that were mostly exposed out of her Fendi skirt. The lotion she'd used had some form of glitter inside of it. It made her skin both pop and smell good. "Nikki, I already know you and Shemar are close and that whenever he is hurting, you are hurting equally. I just wanna let you know I am here for you. You ain't gotta be all tough with me."

She kept driving and simply looked over at me and smiled. Two tears rolled down her cheeks, she wiped them away and kept on rolling. "I love you, boy. Damn, you grew on me fast."

***

Fifteen minutes later, we pulled up the curving driveway of Shemar's palace. He was standing out in front of the white mansion, smoking a cigar. He was dressed in a red robe, that was left open. Underneath was a black tank top, a pair of Supreme shorts and he wore black house shoes.

I got out of Nikki's car, walked over to him, gave him a half hug and patted his back. "What's good, unk?"

He shook his head. "Come on, let me show you something."

I nodded. "A'ight, come on Nikki."

She waved me off. "Nall, you gon' head, I'll be right here."

Shemar looked at her for a second, then continued to lead the way. "Come on, nephew." He stepped up on to the cobbled porch. As soon as he got to the door he paused, took a deep breath and pushed it in.

The first thing I noticed before I even stepped inside of the mansion was the way it smelled. There was the stench of decay. Within three steps inside, I jumped back, right in front of the doorway, about three steps in, was the body of a decapitated woman. She lay on her side, naked and headless. There was a puddle of blood that surrounded her neck. She smelled rank.

"Who the fuck is that?" I asked, frowning my face from both the sheer shock and the scent wafting from her body.

"That was Syndie's sister. Come on."

We stepped over her body and didn't get more than five feet before we were met with two more bodies. One male and one female, both naked and headless. There was so much blood in the hallway that it was slowly making its way in our direction. It had turned a burgundy, black like color.

"That was Syndie, right there and that's her brother." Shemar shook his head and rested against the wall. "Dude was cool as hell and outside of Nikki and Simone. Syndie was a female I really loved." He stared at her body for a long time then started to venture down the hallway.

We had no other choice but to step into the blood. It felt sticky and made a sucking noise as we walked through it. When Shemar got to the end of the hallway and crossed into the grand living room, I started imagining what was coming next. I knew the next person we would see would have to be his daughter Nicole. She was the only one left. So, I followed him into the living room with my head down, when he stopped, I stopped and slowly looked up.

Right in the middle of the floor were the three heads with black bandannas over them, I figured these were the missing heads from the bodies that we'd pasted earlier. Directly in the center of them was Nicole. She had been laid straight out the long way, naked and dismembered. Her arms and legs were separated from her body. From her neck to the tip of her toes were cut up, it was like the killer had pushed her back together as some sick joke. Blood ran in every direction of the living room. Her eyes were wide open.

I couldn't stop looking. "Damn, unk, I'm sorry man. I can only imagine what you're going through."

He dropped to his knees and crawled through the blood to her. Once there, he laid on his side and placed his arm across her body. Then he broke down, crying. That was my cue to go. I felt like one Killa should never be able to watch another Killa cry and lose himself. Since Shemar was something like a mentor to me the sight of him crying hurt my soul, despite the reasoning behind it.

When I got back outside, Nikki was smoking a blunt. She inhaled her smoke and blew it to the sky. "It's fucked up in there, right?"

I nodded. "How do we know that it was the Sinaloas?"

"You can always tell when they make a hit because of the black bandannas they leave at the scene. Besides, this was to be expected. Me and Shemar had to buss a move for, Jefe' Pablo down here in Houston a few weeks ago. We knew they would come back hard. We just didn't fathom they would come back this hard. Poor thing and Nicole just got back in his life. Syndie had been on some pure bullshit for a few years. She finally came around and now this."

Shemar came out of the mansion covered in blood. His eyes were red, he looked sick. "We gotta clap back." He looked from me to Nikki, then back to me again. "These ma'fuckas don't play, JaMichael. Now that you and Phoenix had to bust that move over in Phoenix. You better believe them ma'fuckas gon' holler at you sooner or later. It's best that you get all your ducks in a row. Being in this shit it makes it so hard to love anybody because you can be here today and gone tomorrow, and so can they. Your heart gotta be cold. It's the only chance you got at protecting yourself on all fronts." He wiped his mouth with the back of his hand.

"So, what you wanna do Shemar? You already know I'm down for whatever," Nikki said, walking up to him and rubbing his back.

He dropped his head. "I don't even know, but you best believe I'ma figure it out." He wrapped his arm around Nikki's neck. "They ain't have to take my daughter, Nikki. They ain't have to take my baby. These ma'fuckas playin' a cold game." He started to break down again.

***

Later that night, I was sitting in Nikki's living room sipping on Lean, already fucked up. After seeing all that shit at Shemar's mansion, I just wanted to be numb for a second. I was also silently praying to God I would never have to experience all that he had. I didn't know if I was strong enough to take the kind of loss he had.

Nikki came into the living room and sat on my lap. She turned around facing away from me and leaned her head all the way back on to my shoulder. "JaMichael, you're a big dude. Did you know that?"

I laughed. "Yeah, what makes you say that?"

"I'm just saying." She kissed the side of my cheek. "Baby, do you wanna know something?"

"What's that?"

"I'm tired of this life, JaMichael. I'm tired of having to worry about if I'm going to live or die every single day. I'm tired of worrying about how I'm going to be murdered every single day. I just wanna live happy and free. I wanna break away from these Cartel people. I wish there was a way that we could do that."

"It ain't?"

She shook her head. "Once they get a hold of you, Shemar, they got you for the rest of your natural life." She dropped her head.

"Nall, I ain't finna honor that. Ain't no other man finna tell me what to do with my life. He damn sure ain't finna tell me how my shit gon' end."

"That's exactly what, Jefe' Pablo is banking on. As soon as a ma'fucka sign up to be down with the Cold Heart Cartel, he knows right then and there that their life belongs to him. I wouldn't even be surprised if he already knew how each one of us is going to die. We pretty much living on borrowed time at this point."

I continued to hold her in silence. I imagined Jefe' Pablo sending one of his goons to do to my family what had recently happened to Shemar's, and a cold chill went down my spine. "Ain't nobody ever challenged this dude?"

"What do you mean?" Nikki asked, turning all the way around so that she was straddling me. She had one thick thigh on either side. She wrapped her arms around my neck and looked into my eyes. Sometimes her stares were often intimidating, that was until I'd remember how I be treating her ass in the bedroom, but there was no doubt she was fine as a muthafucka.

"I'm saying the only reason people stay connected to, Jefe' Pablo, is because number one, ain't nobody had the guts to challenge him, and number two, he still has breath in his lungs. If we take this punk's life, then we can break free. As long as we roll under him, we are all just sitting around and waiting for our lives to be taken in a gruesome fashion."

Nikki looked like she was lost in deep thought. "Okay."

"Okay, so how do we penetrate this punk? How do we get close enough to him, to take his ass out?"

She tapped her finger against her chin and clicked her tongue against her teeth. "That's a good question. That man is damn near impossible to get close to. You gotta remember he is worth a billion-plus dollars. That means he has great worth to a whole lot of great and powerful people that will probably make more money with him alive, than dead."

"But on the other hand, you gotta think about it. How many people working under him would really like a new start? How many people are out there are wishing they never got involved with him, to begin with?"

"Probably thousands."

"Right, and I know it has to be some way to use those thousands against him, so we can get close enough to slay his ass. Only, Jefe' Pablo is in control of who belongs to him. If we look at our situation it seems that he has point men."

"Point men, what is that?"

"Well, when he first brought me into this thang, he made sure he placed Shemar as a Point man to me. He told Shemar he was responsible for any rights or wrongs I did. That means this has to be a habit of his. Imagine if we could get some of those Point men on board to go against, Jefe' Pablo? If we could get some of them on boards, we could easily get next to him."

Nikki perked up. "The only person that could get next to him is, Shemar. Jefe' Pablo has a special dinner with those that he has placed in charge every three months. It is then that he breaks down new rules, recruits, and territories, along with agendas, goals, and targets."

"Right, so say Shemar could convince a few of those others to flip with him. We could take out, Jefe' Pablo and start from scratch. We could break away however we wanted, and nobody would be able to tell us shit."

"Ooo, if I wasn't under this man, I would take a long vacation. What would you do, JaMichael?"

"I would work on my manuscripts and get my first series turned in." I missed writing, I had left off in my book on chapter ten. I was half done.

"Wait, boy, you write?"

"Yeah, so does my Pops. I got my inspiration from him."

"JaMichael, are you serious?"

Because if you are, I can plug you with my girl Shawn Walker. Her and my man got this company down in Georgia that's taking the game by storm. If you really wanna handle your bidness on the writing tip, I can have you sit down with her before you go back to Memphis. I'm sure she'll mess with you if you are any good."

"What's the name of their company?" I pulled out my phone.

"Lock Down Publications and Ca$h Presents."

I pulled up the company on my phone and saw the advertisement for all their books. "My pops was telling me about this Cash nigga a few months back. I'ma have to touch bases with him and see what's good, but I'll definitely holla at your homegirl before I bounce. Set that shit up."

"Do you got some of your material on your phone?"

I nodded and pulled it up. "Here, it starts right there."

"Heartless Goon?" She looked at me quizzically. "Am I gon' like it?"

"I don't give a fuck if you do, it's my life uncut, wit' no filter."

"Good, I'ma finna stay up reading it. Unless you want some pussy. I can use some of you, Daddy, if you're up to it."

My phone buzzed right on cue with a text from Bubbie. "N'all, I gotta clear my head. I'm finna hit up Shemar and see if I can get him on board with this Jefe' Pablo shit."

She leaned forward, kissed my lips real soft, and sensual for a full two minutes before she sat back and looked into my eyes. "Before you go back to Memphis you gon' give, Mama, some of this dick. Then we can focus on other shit. You hear me?" She reached between my thighs and squeezed my pipe.

That mama talk coming from her always did something to me. It was like I was under some forbidden spell with her but only when she started talking that shit. I licked her juicy lips, sucking the bottom one into my mouth. "Yeah, Mama, I hear you."

Ghost

Chapter 16

Two weeks passed, still, there was no word from Shemar. Nikki told me that he went underground to pull some strings to see if we could get the ball rolling on Jefe' Pablo. He needed to grease a few palms and make a lot of promises of what life would look like once Jefe' Pablo was out of the mix. I didn't know exactly what all of that entailed, but I took it to mean that Shemar was ready to get Jefe' Pablo out of the way because he was tired of being something like his bitch, just like the rest of us.

Shemar already had the state of Texas behind him. He had so many dope boys, and topnotch kingpins show up to support him at his family's funeral that I'm sure the Feds had a field day taking pictures. They had rolled out the red carpet and had completely shut down the city of Houston. It had been a well put together affair, to say the least, and despite its reasoning for the gathering. Shemar was also supposed to be in charge of finding out who'd been the crew, or persons, responsible for having slain his family. As soon as he found out, Nikki, said he was going to get word to her and me and Phoenix were to handle the culprits immediately. But still, there had been no word as of, yet, and I was anxious.

In the second week, Shemar was still missing in action, I found myself back in Memphis dealing with the dilemma of Danyelle. We were at her mother Veronica's home. Veronica was at work, leaving me and Danyelle alone. Danyelle sat across from me on the couch with her thighs crossed, acting like I wasn't even present, even though she had been the one to call me over. She flipped through the channels and stopped on the *Wendy Williams* show. Then she placed the remote on the couch next to her.

I mugged her for a second, then looked at the clock on my phone and got irritated because I was supposed to be meeting Bubbie in half an hour and the drive from Veronica's house, to Yvonne's was about thirty minutes. "Danyelle, what the fuck you call me over here for?"

She looked over at me and smiled. "Damn, I just ain't seen you in a little while, I was missing you. Why I gotta have some excuse to see you, JaMichael?"

"Because when you hit me up, you said you had something important to show and tell me. Since I was already coming from North Memphis, I figured I'd stop over here. But since you ain't on shit, I'm finna bounce. I gotta go pick Bubbie ass up anyway." I stood up.

She jumped up. "Wait, JaMichael!"

I turned around to look at her. "What's good?"

She walked over to me and stood in my face. She peered into my eyes with her hazel ones. "Baby, I missed you." She ran her hands over my chest, all the way down until she was cuffing my piece. Then she sucked on my neck, she even took the time to bite into the skin there.

I grabbed her wrists and moved her ass back. That shit mighta been feeling good, but I had Bubbie on my mind. We were supposed to been spending some time together as a family after we took the children to the doctor. "Shawty, I ain't got time for that shit, right now. I gotta go make sure my baby mother straight. I'll fuck with you at another time." I turned to leave again.

She waited until I got to the door and called out to me. "JaMichael, you remember, I told you that I was gon' get our little situation taken care of, right?"

I turned around. "Hell yeah, I gave you three gees for that."

"Well—" She lifted her T-shirt and showed me her baby bump.

I frowned and walked back over to her. "That better be because yo' lil' ass just ate something before I came over here." I grabbed her by the shoulders and pushed her against the wall, not hard enough to hurt but to show my displeasure with her hardheaded ass.

"I'm not with hurting our child, JaMichael. You don't gotta say in whether or not this child lives or dies. It's my choice and I choose life, deal with it." She yanked away from me and ran to the back of the house, I heard a door slam.

I stood there rubbing my temples. The more drama I went through with these females, the more I was starting to see that it would be more beneficial for me to simply keep my dick in my pants. I sighed and made my way down the hallway. "Danyelle, let me holla at you for a minute." The house felt like it was too hot like she had the heat up too high. The bulletproof vest was itchy under my black Supreme shirt.

"I ain't got nothing to say to you, JaMichael. You not gonna convince me to get rid of my baby, I'm keeping it."

"You can't do that dumb ass shit! You my lil' cousin, now open the fuckin' door."

"Ain't! And you sho' wasn't worried about me being your cousin when you was doing what you were doing to me. Now all of a sudden it's a problem, you got some nerve."

I tried the lock again. "Danyelle, open this ma'fuckin' door before I kick this bitch in. Stop playin' wit' me. You know I ain't for this bullshit! Open the door lil' cuz!"

"Kiss my ass! Just leave, bye, JaMichael. I'll see yo' punk ass in seven months when I have my child. Yo' black ass better be beside me like you was beside, Bubbie and Tamia stuck up asses. Nigga, what makes them so much better than me? I'm supposed to be yo' blood."

I balled up my fist and punched my hand. "That's the muthafuckin' problem, right there. Open this door. Three—two— I swear to God when I get to one, I'm coming in there and I'm snatching yo' lil' ass up."

"You better fuck me good when you do, too," she spat.

"Bitch! One—two—"

"I don't care!"

"Three!" I took my shoulder and crashed through the door. The lock popped out and fell on the floor. When I came through the threshold, Danyelle was sitting on the edge of the bed hugging a white teddy bear with a red nose to her chest. Her eyes were big as saucers.

"Why the fuck you playin' wit' me, huh?"

"Ain't nobody playin' wit' you. You playin' wit' yo' ma'fuckin' self. I'm having this baby, and that's final."

"Oh, yeah?"

"Yeah."

I rushed her, picked her ass up and sat on the bed. Then turned her over on to her stomach and pulled her over my lap while she kicked her legs wildly. I wrapped my ankle around her two ankles and pulled her coochie cutter shorts up into her ass. "You think shit sweet, right?"

"Let me go! Get off me, JaMichael, I'm tired of you!" She tried the best she could to get away from me.

I brought my hand, high into the air and swung it down as hard as I could, right on her exposed ass cheeks. *Whack*!

She jerked her back and hollered out. "Owwwweeee!"

I didn't give a fuck. "That's what's wrong wit' yo' lil' ass! All a ma'fucka gotta do is smack this ass a lil' bit." *Smack*!

She started to whimper. "Stop, please."

Smack! Smack! Smack! Smack! My hand went right to work on her naked ass, back to back with no regard. She kicked her legs best she could and hollered out in pain. I made

136

sure her shorts were pulled out up on her ass so I could get them cheeks. In a matter of minutes, her ass was red and glowing, I let her go.

She stood in front of me with tears coming down her cheeks. She dropped her shorts and started rubbing her ass over her panties. I noticed that the front of her panties was in her crotch and they were soaked in her juices.

"I hate you, JaMichael. Why you do that to me?" She switched from one foot to the next. Her panties traveled further upward into her sex.

"You so ma'fuckin' hardheaded. I told you what to do with that money, you was supposed to do it."

"But I just love you like they do. I don't care what you are to me. I want to have a piece of you just like they do. Damn, and you do me like this." She blinked and more tears fell from her eyes.

I grabbed her by the waist and pulled her to me. My face was right by her pussy. I could smell a hint of her and everything. One of her yellow lips were showing. I saw that her inner thighs were glistening with her juices. "I'm sorry man, I ain't mean to hit you."

"But you did, though." She continued to rub her ass. I caught the view of what she was really doing from the mirror that hung on the door. Both of her ass cheeks were outside of her panties. "I thought you loved me, cuz?" She stepped forward and rested her hands on my shoulders.

Now her pussy was right in my face, I lost all control. I kissed her fat lips through the panties and licked up and down the crack.

She stood on her tippy toes and tossed her head back. "JaMichael, ooo! Can you spank me again? Please!"

I pulled her leg back to the side and sucked her lips into my mouth. While my tongue shot in between her gap. "You fuckin' me up, Danyelle. Damn, I'm tryna get shit right wit', Bubbie." I opened her lips wide and sucked on her pearl, while she humped into my face.

"Uh-uh, so—so, cuz, I don't care. I want you, too." She placed her foot on the bed and really started riding my tongue while I slurped away."

She musta humped away on me for about ten minutes. The next thing I knew she was cumming hard and I was bending her ass over the bed, sliding in her from the back. Her panties were around one of her ankles. I was fuckin' her as hard as I could, holding onto her hips, smacking her ass at the same time.

"Gimme this forbidden shit. Tell me you love cuz dick!"

"Uh, uh, uh! Yes, ooo, JaMichael—please!" She pushed back on me as hard as she could over and over.

Her cat was tight and juicy. Every time I smacked that ass, she seemed to spit on me inside her womb. She made me get aggressive, I grabbed a handful of her hair and pulled her head back while I hit that pussy hard from the back, smacking that juicy ass the whole way.

She placed her face in the bed and tilted her ass up, that's how Veronica found us. "What the fuck are y'all doing in my house!" she snapped.

I came hard inside of Danyelle and pulled my piece out at the same time it was still going off. Cum spit all over Danyelle's ass and lower back. When I turned around to face Veronica a trail of semen leaked from my piece. "Veronica, I can explain."

She rushed me and slapped my face. "The fuck is wrong wit' you? That's my daughter!"

Danyelle scooted back on the bed and grabbed the sheets. She wrapped them around her body. "Mama, I'm sorry, but I love, JaMichael. I have always loved him, please don't be mad."

Veronica didn't say a word, she sidestepped me and dove onto the bed. "You lil' bitch I'm finna kill you, I'm over you!"

Danyelle screamed and jumped up. "Stop! Stop, I'm pregnant, I'm pregnant! You gon' hurt my baby."

Veronica stopped in her tracks, looking dumbfounded. "*Pregnant?*"

She looked at me. "JaMichael, who is she pregnant by?"

I stood up and fixed my pants. "T.T., come on now. We ain't finna do this, right now."

"JaMichael, who the fuck is my little daughter pregnant by?"

"Veronica, I can explain," I started.

"*You* mean to tell me, you got my baby pregnant? You of all people!" She rushed me swinging wildly.

I caught her, picked her up and slammed her on to the bed, pinning her there. "Man, calm yo' ass down. Now I can explain everything, just listen to me."

She jerked away and pushed me. She ran her fingers through her hair. She looked from me to Danyelle and back to me. "Nall, muthafucka, you listen to me. I want you to take this bitch, and all her stuff, along with yourself and anything you might have in my house and I want y'all out of here. I'm giving you half an hour, matter fact, scratch that, I'm giving you ten minutes to get out of my house and off my property. If the tenth minute comes and either of you are still here, I'm killing you. The time starts now!" She looked at her watch and walked out of the room.

"But, mama!" Danyelle cried.

"You're dead to me lil' girl," Veronica hollered and walked out of the room in a Zombie-like fashion.

I stood there perplexed, but when those ten minutes came, me and Danyelle were no longer in the vicinity of her home. We were headed to a hotel until I could figure out how I was going to explain all of this to Bubbie.

Chapter 17

"JaMichael, I love you, but I can't do this no more," were the first words out of her mouth, as soon as I explained to Bubbie the situation between me and Danyelle and what had taken place with Veronica.

"You can't do what no more?" I asked, getting up from the bed, standing over her in the den of her mother's home.

"This shit between me and you. I've tried and tried. I just don't see how things can possibly work between us. It was one thing when Tamia popped up pregnant. That alone made me want to break away from you, but now you telling me, Danyelle is about to have your baby, too? That's your people. That's just too weird. I know how people get down behind closed doors here in Memphis and that's fine, to each its owns but when it hit close to home like this, it's just—too much for me to handle. I'm sorry!" She stood up and grabbed her coat, sliding it on her shoulders. "I do wish you the best, though."

She hugged me and made her way toward the front door. I rushed ahead of her and closed it back. "Don't leave me, Bubbie. Please lil' Mama I'm begging you as a man. "

"JaMichael, there is nothing more I can do here. You got a baby on the way by your whole ass cousin. You already got one by, Tamia. Ain't no telling how many other kids you got out there. I don't want my twins being subjected to this kind of dysfunction. I'm sorry, now that they are here, they are my first priorities. That's just the way it is."

"Those are my kids, too, Bubbie. I love them just as much as you do. I'm not about to let you break up our family."

"You're breaking up our family, JaMichael. Ain't nobody else doing it but you. So, stop with that bullshit. You're look-ing for somewhere else to point the finger instead of right at yourself. Now I wish I could, but I can't, and you just gon' have to accept that." She reached for the door again.

I moved her hand out of the way. "Bubbie, I'm not finna lose you. I promise I'll never fuck around on you again. I'ma do right by you, from here on out it's gon' be all about you and our boys. That's on my heart." I crossed it with the sign of the crucifix.

"You know what, JaMichael? I mighta been dumb enough to believe that if you actually had a heart, but seeing as I know that you don't, I don't believe a word coming out of your fuckin' mouth. Now please get the fuck out of my way, it's over."

I pulled her from the door and tossed her on the bed. She bounced twice and sat up, looking pissed. "Bubbie, you need to listen to me. I know I done said some shit before and I might not have meant it, but this time I really do. I swear on my mother's grave, I'ma do everything I can as a man to hold you down like I'm supposed too. Fuck the cheating. Fuck putting anybody, or anything outside of our family before you. You got my word as a man on that. All I'm asking is that you give me a chance. Please try and trust me, I'm begging you, baby." I pulled her up and wrapped my arms around her.

She stayed slack for a few moments. Then she tilted her head back and sighed out loud. "JaMichael, we can't keep doing this. You can't keep dragging me in the same circle over and over again. It's not fair. You have to stand up and be a man. So far you have been nothing more than a coward. You ain't owned up to nothing and if I keep on cutting you slack, what kind of an example am I setting for our boys?"

I took a step back and took a hold of her hands. "I know baby, but please, you gotta just trust me this time. All that shit is out of my system. I know that I want to be with you faithfully. I know you are supposed to be my wife, I'm sure now,

142

Bubbie." I went into my pocket and pulled out the box that the three-carat, pink lemonade, diamond ring was inside. Then lowered to one knee.

Bubbie mugged me and looked toward the ceiling. "What are you doing, JaMichael?"

"Look, Bubbie." I opened the box to show her the contents.

Her eyes lit up. The diamond glistened in the light. "What is that?"

"Baby, I know I been fucking up. I know I ain't been doing right by you, or our babies yet, but I need you to know that I love you. I'm in love with you and I want—no scratch that, I need you to be my wife. I always told Jahliya that when I got married, I would never cheat on my wife. That I would always do right by her. I need you to be my wife, so you can take me from these streets. Take me from this game and these other bitches. All I care about is you, Bubbie."

She kept her head tilted back until tears came from each side of her eyes. "Why are you doing this to me?"

"Please, Kalissa Shande' Dostier, will you be my wife? Can you rescue me from this hell I'm swimming in?"

She shook her head. "You got a baby on the way by, Danyelle. JaMichael, how is that going to work?"

"I'm gon' talk her into doing the right thing. Even if I gotta cash her ass out. Don't worry about this, Bubbie."

"I can't help but, too. Are you still gon' be sleeping with her? You know, behind my back, and all that shit?"

"Never again, only you lil' Mama, I promise."

"What about, Tamia?"

"Fuck her, she don't exist. If it ain't about, Taurus, I ain't gon' have no dealings with her. If I do I'll make sure you're right in the mix of everything. I won't keep nothing from you, I promise."

"And any other bitch in the streets, what about them?"

I pulled her down until she was on her knees with me. "I promise, it's just you from here on out, Bubbie. I just wanna make you happy." I rested my lips against her forehead.

She held out her fingers. "It, better fit."

I smiled and breathed a sigh of relief at the same time. "Is that a yes, baby? Please say that's a yes!"

"Yes, Daddy, but you better keep your word because I ain't gon' forget none of what you said tonight."

I howled, slid the ring on to her finger and picked her up in the air. "Yes, I'm so happy!"

She started laughing as I turned her around and around in a circle. "Stop it, Daddy, you gon' make me dizzy."

Yvonne opened the door to the bedroom with both twins, she had one on each hip, their little curls were popping. "What the hell is going on in here?"

"Were engaged, Mama. JaMichael, bought me a big ring and he promises not to cheat on me no more. Isn't that what's up?"

"Sound like my life all over again, Kalissa. I just hope he stands by his word more than your father did." She looked over at me. "Congratulations, these kids deserve parents that are living in wedlock." She paused. "I gotta finish giving them their bath." She stepped back into the hallway and closed the door.

***

I don't know what was going on with Shemar, but over the next few weeks, I continued to keep in touch with Nikki, all while hustling as hard as I could. Shemar was missing in action. Nikki said he'd taken about thirty niggas with him down to Mexico, and he only checked in with her every now and then. I didn't understand what that was about, but as far as I was concerned, he was an old head in the game. I figured he knew how to navigate through the slums and the underworld. I was taking the position that I would be ready to go as soon as he called my number.

Not only had my troops fully taken over the Orange Mound district, but we moved Northward, and fully conquered the Frayser district as well. Before we were able to do that, the district was ridden with some mediocre, nobody ass, block boys that were playin' wit' peanuts. Ain't none of them ma'fuckas really have no blue faces. The Heartless Goon Cartel started airing at their asses every chance we got and even slayed a few before they got the message to move around altogether.

I still wasn't fucking wit' that nigga Phoenix like that. As far as I was concerned, he was still salty for how we had taken over his strip and moved him Southward toward White Haven, though all the locals like myself had renamed that district, we called it Black Haven. Phoenix took to that area and really went hard. He opened traps on damn near every block and flooded it with Jefe' Pablo's Tar. The only time we really connected was when we handled bidness in the other cities in Tennessee. I had to make sure he was on top of his game because as long as Jefe' Pablo was in power our lives rode on meeting his monthly set quotas. I was tired of that shit, but in order to do what I needed to do, I played by the rules of the Cold Heart Cartel.

In addition to getting my footing in the game, I followed Nikki's advice and linked up with this sistah, Shawn Walker. Well, should I say she linked up with me? It was three weeks to the day that I had seen Shemar last when Nikki hit my phone at one o'clock in the afternoon. I was rolling with Bubbie in the passenger's seat of my red Porsche. As soon as my phone rang, she picked it up and looked at the face. I knew something wasn't right when she grunted.

"Uh, JaMichael, who the fuck is Shawn? It, betta be a nigga and even then, today is family day." We were on our way to, Cooper Young, so we could take the kids to the Zoo.

I kept rolling. "Let me get that, it's important."

"Ain't, we made a deal. If it's anybody calling this phone that I don't know we putting it on speaker. That way me, you and our sons can hear who is on the other line. So, here we go, I'm finna flip it on speaker, right now." She did.

"Hello, JaMichael?" Came Nikki's voice.

"What up, Mama?"

"Nothing lil' daddy, how you doing, baby?" Nikki asked.

"*Baby*, uh, excuse me the only person that's supposed to be calling him *baby* is me," Bubbie interrupted.

"Who the hell is that, JaMichael?" Nikki snapped. "She rude as hell."

"Rude, bitch?" Bubbie grabbed the phone and put it to her mouth. I was doing all I could to switch lanes and grab it back from her.

"Bitch, who you calling a bitch?" Nikki inquired. "Where is my lil' daddy?"

"Uh, this is his wife to be, Bubbie, can you please call him by his name? All those terms of endearments are reserved for me and only me. Now, who the fuck are you?"

"Gimme the phone, Bubbie," I snapped. "That's my homie, she's like my mother. Stop playing and shit!"

"Ain't." She moved the phone out of reach. "Go ahead, I'm listening! Who are you?"

"Look, lil' girl, I am a grown-ass woman. I ain't got time for yo' games. Lil' Daddy, Shawn is in town, she wanna meet you. I sent her over three of those books you wrote and we talking about checking you a bag, right now. When she hit you, get up with her, and don't make me look bad. I love you, peace." She hung up.

"She loves you! Boy, JaMichael, this bitch finna get you fucked up," Bubbie threatened.

"Man, you tripping. I told you Shawty like my moms. She in her late thirties, early forties, and all that shit. You see what she talking about."

"Anyway, are you serious about pursuing the writing thing?" Bubbie asked, looking out of her window.

I nodded. "Even though I been in the streets, I been writing every night on my iPad. I can't stop, I done finished six books already. I even got you in three of them." I snickered at that.

"Me?"

"Yep, so ma'fuckas gon' know how you be chewing all on daddy. If it's one thing for sure they gon' be like Bubbie got some stupid head."

She reached over and slapped my shoulder. "You better change my name, JaMichael. What if my mother read that book?"

"She gon' be proud of you." I busted up laughing.

She just kept smacking me all over, hitting me anywhere she could. "I'm so sick of yo' shit, boy." Then she sat back in her seat and crossed her arms.

"I'm just playing, baby, but yeah, I'm finna leave this game alone, and jump into that book game, depending on what Shawn and this nigga, Ca$h, my Pops was talking about, on. If I can get that real cheese from doing that, then I'ma just do that. I gotta get on my grown man shit and find other ways to provide a life for you and our babies."

"What about school, are you planning on going to college still? Cause I am. I wanna study business and get me a degree in Early Childhood Education."

"Yeah, but that's down the road. For now, I got a few messes to clean up." My phone started buzzing and I saw right away that it was a number out of Texas because Bubbie flashed the face to me.

"Baby, that can be, Shawn, right there because I don't recognize the number. Pick it up and don't be on none of that disrespectful shit. Keep in mind it could be bidness."

"Shut up, you act like I ain't got good sense. I know what I gotta do, and how to conduct myself." She hit the speaker button. "Hello?"

"Hello, my name is, Shawn Walker. May I speak with, Ja-Michael Stevens, please?"

Bubbie pushed the phone closer to my ear. "Here he go."

"JaMichael, are you there?"

"Yeah, I'm just pulling over, hold on." I pulled over the Porsche about a hundred yards away from the lakefront. "A'ight, how you doin' sistah?"

"I'm fine, and what about yourself?"

"Peaceful, what's good?"

"Well, my close friend, Nikki, submitted three of your manuscripts for possible publishing. They are titled Raised As A Goon. Was publishing something you were thinking about?"

"Hell yeah!" Bubbie hollered over my shoulder.

I nudged her lil' ass back and mugged her. "I'm sorry about that."

"He got two whole ass kids in the back. Y'all need to help him leave them streets alone. Hell yeah, we seeking publishing. He got six books done in all, cash us out!"

Shawn started cracking up on the phone. "Excuse me?"

I got out of the Porsche with the phone to my ear. "Don't mind her. That's my baby mother, she tripping."

"And yo' Fiancée, don't forget about that!" Bubbie hollered so loud, that the twins started screaming.

I walked a short distance away from the Porsche. "Anyway, yeah, I'm interested in turning over a new leaf. How do we get started?"

"Well, that's good. Actually, I'm already in town. I'm in the Orange Mound at the Wing Factory. I'm just pulling up. So, if you'll meet me there in twenty minutes, we can discuss your possible contract, and what we can do for you."

"Look, Shawn, before we even do all that. I'm a dope boy, I'm 'bout my paper. I need to know if I'ma check a bag upfront?"

"Well, just based on what we've read, I'll say upon signing to us, you could walk away with a substantial amount before your first book even comes out. But let's discuss that more over lunch. Cool?"

"As a breeze off the lake, I'll be there."

Ghost

Chapter 18

The first thing I noticed about, Shawn was that she had a real strong southern accent, yet, she spoke with proper English. She was about five-feet-five inches tall and brown-skinned, with a beautiful face and alluring eyes. She carried herself with an aura of confidence and uniqueness. I was a straight street nigga and even though she was talking a bunch of legal mumbo jumbo, I couldn't help but tune into her every word like Netflix, while I ate a few pieces of chicken off my plate. For some reason my twins were acting up, so after, Bubbie met Shawn face to face she excused herself and went to wait in the Porsche. She told us that we had a half-hour to talk and insisted I kept my phone on speaker so she could hear everything. Shawn said it wasn't a problem and even commended her for standing on me as a Queen before she walked out of the door.

Fifteen minutes later, I'd gotten Shawn's best pitch. "So, that's basically what we can offer you, right there. You're guaranteed to have your books in all the top bestselling magazines in the urban community, as well as online and in all the major and minor bookstores. We're talking Barnes and Noble, Amazon, and Ingram. I can honestly say that with a little work you'll be able to live just like you're still a dope boy. We'll make sure of that because at LDP we chase that paper."

I nodded, I liked hearing that. "That's what's up, I'm in."

"Great." Shawn smiled, she was fine, I had to give that sistah her props. "We're family here. So, if there is ever anything you need outside of the business side of things you should never hesitate to call me on this number or this one. My emails and Facebook are also on this card. If I can just get your email, I'll send over the contract as soon as I go over a few things with Ca$h."

That sounded like a plan, I typed my information into her phone. "I'm really trying to turn my life around, sis. You see that lil' family I got out, they're depending on me."

She smiled and looked into my eyes again. I had to look off, that penetrating stare was too much for a young nigga like me that was trying to be one hunnit to Bubbie. I was seconds away from relapsing and trying to see what Shawty fine ass was really on. "Well, we'll do our part, as long as you're willing to do yours."

I peeped her fingers to see if she had a wedding ring on or something like that. I was surprised when I didn't see one. "So, are you and Ca$h together?"

She laughed and fixed a tuft of hair behind her ear. "Nall, we're business partners. We started from the bottom together." She looked off as if in a zone. "I love him."

I nodded. "That's what's up. Well, I guess I'll be in touch when you send over that contract." I scooted my chair back and stood up, wiping my hands on a wet wipe before extending it to her.

She smiled that gorgeous smile again, then she covered her mouth with her hand. "Oh my God, JaMichael, look." She pointed outside.

Four dudes had surrounded my Porsche with black masks covering their faces. One of them I saw had a gun in his hand. I grabbed my phone and ran out the door. Before I was twenty steps from the restaurant, I had my gun out and aiming. *Bocka! Bocka! Bocka! Bocka!* The shells jumped out of the gun. One of the dudes fell, jumped up and took off running.

All four separated and ran in different ways. The one with the gun stopped, aimed and fired. *Boom! Boom! Boom!* I felt two bullets crash into my chest and knock me back. He jiggled the handle of the Porsche and tried to get inside of the car. I could hear Bubbie screaming on the inside and on my phone which was still on speaker.

"Open the door, bitch!"

I'd fallen to one knee, now I was back up and bucking. *Bocka! Bocka! Bocka!*

He fell back and held his shoulder, dropping the gun. He thought about picking it up when Bubbie opened the door and popped him twice in the chest. *Bloom! Bloom!* He fell sideways and started shaking on the pavement.

I got to him just as she was slamming the door. I stood over him and went berserk. *Bocka! Bocka! Bocka!* His body jumped over and over. I picked him up and stuffed him into the passenger's side of our car, then I jumped into the driver's seat and stormed away.

***

"Just a few more feet lil' Mama. We walked sideways until we got to the bridge, then Bubbie helped me hoist the garbage can filled with the Shooter's ashes up on to the ledge of the overpass, so I could dump it over. His remains emitted a smoky cloud, then sunk to the bottom of the Alligator infested creek. It was pitch black outside the swamp, the only light that illuminated the water came from that of the moon.

Bubbie came over to me and placed her arm around my waist. "Damn, Daddy, how many times have you had to do a nigga like this?" she asked, looking into the water.

"Too many times to count, baby. Sometimes this just the way the game gotta go. Fuck that nigga."

"Yeah, I agree. But do you think you killed him? Or did I do it?" she asked looking up at me, swatting away a Mosquito.

I didn't want her having that shit on her conscious, so I didn't care if she had been the one to do it or not, I had to take that burden. "When I ran up on dude he was still breathing. That's why I had to finish him."

"Ah." She looked in the water again. "Daddy, it seems like you are always in the right place at the right time when it comes to protecting me. I love you so much, I hope you know that. Do you?"

I kissed her forehead. "Of, course I do, that's why you the wife."

"We still gotta get it on paper, though. My mama said it's too many dumb females out there claiming to be a man's wife, but they never put that shit on paper. When it all boils down and that man comes up, he really don't owe them a damn thing. That's not gon' be us. You gon' marry me so I can be all up in yo' pockets when those books drop. I know you gon' be successful." She kissed my cheek. "Thank you for saving me, Daddy."

I held her under my arm and felt complete. "I love you, too, boo."

"Daddy, is your chest okay?"

"It's good, I'ma have you rub some solution on it when we get home. Come on, let's get the fuck up out of here."

***

That night me and Bubbie cuddled up in the bed and listened to *Jhenè Aiko*. She seemed to love her for some reason, the more I listened to her the more she began to grow on me as well. She felt so good in my arms. I was laying on my back, and she was laying on top of me.

"Daddy, do you really think we're going to be able to leave the slums alone and venture off into something positive? Aren't you in love with the streets?"

I took a deep breath and exhaled slowly. I had her ass gripped in my big hands. It felt good to me. "Baby, I love the slums, but since our children are born, I know I gotta get up out of them. I gotta get us to a better place. I'm fuckin' wit' Cartels and dope boys, bodying niggas and all types of shit. How the fuck am I gon' raise a family getting down like this?"

Bubbie shrugged her shoulders. "I don't know, Daddy. I really hope you pursue this writing stuff. I'll even help you, I love reading those hood books. I think I might even have a novel in me. Who knows?"

"Well, I hope you write it so I can check that bag," I joked kissing her forehead.

"Yeah, right, you already know I'm 'bout my paper. I'm the only Gold Digger in this relationship and rightfully so. I pushed out two of yo' kids. That gives me the right to run the show for the rest of our lives. Y'all heads ain't little for the record, baby." She snickered. "But I trust you to hold us down, Daddy. I believe in you I also got some more news that might throw you a little bit of a curveball."

I rubbed her ass and squeezed it. "Oh, yeah, what's that?"

She sighed. "I don't know what you been eating but—" She stood up and opened the top drawer to her dresser. When she came back, she handed me three positive pregnancy tests. "But I'm pregnant again, so you best be hollering at Danyelle."

My eyes bucked. "Fuck, I was supposed to meet her in Black Haven, she supposed to be flying back to South Carolina in three hours."

Bubbie looked stunned. "You better hurry up? What she finna do with the baby?"

"I don't know but I'll be back." I jumped up and hit it out of there as fast as I could.

***

When I got back to the hotel, Danyelle was busy packing her suitcase. She didn't even acknowledge me when I came through the door. She simply looked back at me and kept doing what she was doing. I eased inside the suite and closed the door behind me. I peeked out the window that was on the side of the balcony to see what I could see. I had my security downstairs, roaming throughout the parking lot. I was paranoid as a muthafucka and didn't even know why.

Danyelle cleared her throat. "I talked to Tamia today. We had a long conversation about, you and Bubbie."

"Is that right?" I asked, sitting on the side of the bed.

She continued to pack. "Yeah, we was trying to figure out why it is that you chose, Bubbie over either one of us? I mean I know why you chose her over me obviously, but what about Tamia or any other bad bitch out there? She ain't all that?" She grunted and curled her lip at me.

I ignored that dumb shit. "Danyelle, what out the baby?"

"What about it?"

"What you finna do with it? Ain't yo' pops gon' wanna know who it is?"

She sucked her teeth. "Aw, he already knows my mother made sure of that. She ain't had a decent conversation with that man in over ten years, but you should've heard them two on the phone. They were having a real good time. She invited me in her home long enough for me to hear that. It was so irritating. I forgot why I even let you fuck me in the first place." She stood there for a minute lost in deep thought.

"Danyelle, who gives a fuck? You can't have this baby."

"Why, JaMichael, why can't I have this baby? It ain't gon' be no more fucked up than you or me. Our roots are twisted. It don't matter who we have kids by." She walked past me and opened the closet door, then stopped and turned around.

"Ghost, I just wanna let you know that I do love you and if I can't have you then can't none of these other bitches have you either." She grabbed her clothes off the hangers and tossed them on to the bed.

I came closer to her. "What the fuck you mean by that?"

"You'll see." She stuffed the clothes into the suitcases and closed it best she could. Then she climbed on to the bed and sat on the suitcase, zipping it up.

I grabbed a handful of her long ass hair and pulled her back to me. "What the fuck does that mean?"

"Ow, let me go. You always handling me all rough, that's how I know you really don't care about me," she whined.

I grabbed her hair firmer. "What did you mean by that?"

"Nothing, it's just that, Tamia told me about what happened with Chino and Jessie. She told me how you bodied both of them and that, Erica her friend witnessed it all. You did it because you were jealous of her and Chino. That's ridiculous. How come you ain't never been jealous over me before?" she asked, looking at me with her head turned sideways.

"Man, Tamia, lying like a ma'fucka. When have you ever known for me to be jealous over any dude?" I couldn't believe she would tell my cousin some shit like that, when in actuality, Tamia had been the one to body both Jessie and Chino. I hadn't even gotten the chance to do either, but I would never tell Danyelle that. "So, you saying her friend Erica backing her story, too, huh?"

Danyelle shrugged her shoulders. "I don't know, that's what she say. As far as you being jealous over another dude, how would I know that? You barely took me anywhere." She grabbed another bag and placed it on top of the bed. "I swear, you and I could've had a great life together. This is the South that shit wouldn't have been as uncommon as you think. All we should've done was moved the fuck out of Memphis, but I knew you wouldn't do that for me. The only person you would ever move for is, Bubbie. That's fucked up, JaMichael." She grabbed all her stuff and headed toward the door. "Oh, and don't worry about the baby. My father already said when I get to South Carolina he's going to make sure it's taken care of." She did little air quotes with her fingers. "You can go live your best life. You never know how short that best life may be these days."

The next thing I knew there was a horn sounding downstairs and she was leaving the room, then was gone. I didn't even try to stop her. I watched her drive away in the Uber. As soon as she was gone, I sat on the edge of the bed and lowered my head. I couldn't believe Tamia. What the fuck was she trying to promote about me? I needed to get over there to her, quick. On my way out the door my phone buzzed. As soon as I read the face, I got chills.

Chapter 19

"Tamia, I'm not gon' ask you this shit again. Who did this to your face?" I grabbed her and held her shoulders. She had a black eye and busted lips. Her head looked like she'd been beaten severely. I was pissed off, I didn't give a fuck what I was going through with my baby mother. Wasn't no nigga about to put his hands on her and fuck her up like somebody had, she looked horrible.

She jerked away from me and pushed me out of her battered face. "JaMichael, why you acting like you care about me all of a sudden?" she slurred and held the towel that had been dipped in ice water to her lips. "You ain't been caring about me this long." She walked over, sat on the couch, grabbed a blunt out of the ashtray and sparked it.

I came into the living room and looked down at her. "What the fuck are you talking about? Who did this shit to your face Tamia?"

"After all that shit, we went through as kids, JaMichael. After all, the struggling together and holding each other in the freezing cold when both of our electricity and gas was out at home. After all, the promises we made to each other and all the love we confessed for and about each other. Why would you go and leave me for some bitch that ain't did nothing but hated on me since I knew her? That bitch had everything handed to her and we struggled together. Yet, you chose her over me! What's the matter with you, Ghost?" she screamed.

I looked both ways, then down at her. We were in a small, one-bedroom apartment, in North Memphis. The neighborhood was predominantly white folks with a very low crime rate. I already knew any loud outbursts or screaming like she was doing could potentially cause the police to be called.

"Tamia, I ain't choose nobody over you. Me and Bubbie are figuring things out. She got two of my sons. She been doing the best she can to hold me down since all that shit kicked off with, Jahliya. We just grew close over time. I ain't ask for this shit to happen."

She stood up and blew a cloud of smoke into my face. "It's always all about you, JaMichael. All you care about is you. You don't give a fuck about me. You don't really give a fuck about, Bubbie or these kids we pushed out for your big-headed ass. All you truly care about is you. Yousa selfish bastard and if I was a man, I would kick yo' ass." She sat back on the couch, set her blunt in the ashtray, picked up her phone, and started texting. "Yousa bitch, JaMichael. That's all you are and all you'll ever be." She shook her head and kept texting.

I stood there mugging her for a hot minute. That bitch had my mind all fucked up. I couldn't believe she was talking to me like she was. It seemed as if she were losing her mind. "What the fuck is wrong with you?"

She looked me over. "Nigga, you are what's wrong with me. You got my mind all fucked up and shit. You see, I thought you really loved me, JaMichael. I thought it was going to be me, and you forever, but now look. Why the fuck would you save me?" She stood back up and stepped into my face. I could smell the liquor on her breath now.

"What the fuck is you talking about, Shawty? Save you from what?"

"From, Chino. Why would you bring yo' ass way across town to save me from him? When you really didn't want to be with me? Hell, if I'd knew you didn't want me I could've stayed with him. But now you kilt him and my best friend, all for what?" she screamed.

I closed the distance between us and covered her mouth with my right hand. "Bitch, stop all that ma'fuckin' hollering before one of these people call the police. What the fuck is wrong with you? Are you stupid or somethin?"

She broke free of me and backed up. "I loved Chino, Ja-Michael. You didn't have to kill him. You didn't have to take him away from me if you weren't going to be with me. That's not fair and you had no right killing, Jessie."

"Bitch what?" Tamia was tripping, I didn't understand it.

How the fuck was she saying I had killed two people that she in fact had. All I'd done was beat the fuck out of Chino after he called himself trying to pistol-whip Tamia. Jessie, her so-called friend, had Chino's gun, Jessie tried her best to buck me down, but the gun wound up being on safety and apparently, she didn't know how to work it. Tamia got a hold of her, they fought for a short time and somehow, someway, Jessie, wound up with a knife in her throat. That was before Tamia had taken the gun from Jessie and aired Chino out with it. Yeah, Tamia had to be losing her mind.

"I don't want your baby, JaMichael. I hate that baby and I hate your guts. As far as I'm concerned that baby ain't gon' do nothing but turn into a rotten, dirty, killer like you." She picked up the pillow from the couch and threw it at me.

Suddenly it dawned on me. Since I had been there, I had not seen my son, Taurus. I looked around the room. "Tamia, where the fuck is my son?"

She broke into a fit of laughter. "Aw, now you worried about him?" She waved me off? "Boy, bye."

I rushed that bitch and pinned her ass against the wall. "Where the fuck is my son?"

She closed her eyes and smiled. "This the most action I don' got from yo' ass in weeks. It feels good, too." She exhaled, then slowly opened her eyelids. "Ahhhhh! Ahhhh! Help me—help me, he's trying to kill me!"

I placed my hand over her mouth. "Where the fuck is my son, Tamia?"

She cocked back her leg and kicked me right in the nuts hard as she could, buckling me. I fell to my knees, then to my side. "That muthafucka better know how to swim." She started cracking up. "I hate you, JaMichael! You killed my friends." She kicked me in the side as I was trying to get up, then she ran and disappeared down the hall, screaming at the top of her lungs.

I struggled to come to my feet. I had to rest against the wall. It felt like my balls were in my stomach and like I had to throw up. When I finally gained my composure, I took off down the hall behind her. When I was two steps inside of the hall, she opened the bathroom door and slung Taurus out of it. I mean she threw him in the air. "Here, take his lil' bitch ass. I hate him, too!"

I don't know how I managed to do it, but as he was floating through the air I tripped over my own fuckin' feet from being caught off guard by her sheer madness and dove, catching him at the same time my elbows bumped against the gray carpet. He was wet and appeared to not be breathing. His eyes were wide open.

"Ha, ha, po' baby. Fuck him!" She slammed the bathroom door. As soon as it was closed, she opened it and ran into the bedroom.

I laid my son on his back. Tears started coming out of my eyes. "Damn, Taurus, please man." I tapped his cheek, then lowered my head to his chest to see if I could hear a heartbeat. Before I could get my ear on it good enough.

Tamia ran out of the bedroom naked, with a shotgun. I stood right up. "You finna die, JaMichael. It's time to meet yo' muthafuckin' maker." She pumped it and aimed the barrel at my head. "Say yo' prayers you silly, rabbit." She started cracking up again, then flipped serious.

I held up my hands. "Tamia, what the fuck is wrong with you?"

"Say yo' prayers, Ghost! Say em, say now I lay me down to sleep! Say it—say it—say it, ahhhh!" she hollered.

She aimed the shotgun and placed her finger on the trigger, as tears ran down her face. I dropped my head and rushed her as fast as I could. *Boom!* The shotgun went off at the same time the police rushed into the apartment, every bit of twenty deep. They had on masks and tactical equipment. Before I knew it, we were being bum-rushed.

***

Six months later, Bubbie sat across the visiting table from me. She held my hand and wiped her tears with a Kleenex. "That bitch bogus, Daddy. She admitted to Jessie's murder and the attempt on Taurus's life. She still swears you are the one that bodied, Chino. How the fuck did she get your gun to be able to turn it into these people?"

I shook my head. "I still don't know, but all they got is her word against mine, right?"

She nodded. "Yeah, and it helped that they found out she was on that PCP real tough. You didn't know she was on that either?"

"N'all, Chino must've turned her on that, too. He stayed fuckin' around in D.C." I slammed my fist on the table. "What my lawyer saying?"

Bubbie smiled. "He says you're going to beat this shit. They ain't got nothing on you but her word. They done already caught her in more lies, than Donald Trump. Cassius Alexander and Shawn Walker dropped a hundred bands for one of the best attorneys in Memphis. You'll meet with him tomorrow. They say they'll be flying out to see you in a month or so and to keep writing that uncut shit with no filter. The streets eating it up, I'm proud of you, Daddy."

"This shit coming natural, baby. I can't sleep, I'm up writing all hours of the night like an insomniac. I been through so much shit. But make sure you send my gratitude to both of them and let 'em know I'ma keep doing my thing."

"Will do. Oh, and they sent you a few bands through Access for your commissary. You should be straight for a minute."

"What about you, you got that bag I left?"

She nodded. "Yeah, I didn't know you had so much money put up. Then again I shouldn't have ever underestimated you, to begin with."

"You know that." I tightened my grip on her hand. "Baby, you know I'm finna come from under this don't you?"

"There is no doubt in my mind that you are. I'ma be right here by your side when you do, ten toes down." She looked into my eyes and exhaled. "Jahliya, pregnant, I ain't gon' tell you by who because you gon' flip. Danyelle had the baby, it's a girl, as far as I know, her mother Veronica said it came out very healthy and beautiful, with hazel eyes like her. She sends her love, so does Jahliya. They will be out to see you soon. Shemar handled his bidness and Nikki said to tell you that you are free, just come from under that situation, to let her know what you need, she got you. Shemar says the same. My mother says she knew you wasn't nothing but a finer version of my father." She rolled her eyes. "Whatever." She squeezed my hand. "I miss you, Daddy. I'm going crazy without you. I can't wait until this is over."

"Hey, hey, hey. You gotta be strong, lil' Mama, I got this. I'll be home to my baby girl real soon. Who's my, Baby Girl?"

"Me."

"And who do I love more than anybody else?"

"Me." She wiped her tears away.

***

A year later I wound up finally beating both bodies. They hit me with felony possession of a firearm and gave me five years in the Feds. Yeah, Tennessee, plays a dirty game, but the way I see it, shit could've been a lot worst. Bubbie been holding me down ever since. That's my Baby Girl, right there. She stays on me so that I write at least three books a month on this real-life shit. All my writing got no filters. I write it like I remember it, and I am who I am. Twenty-twenty is my year. Free the real. Ghost!

The End

Submission Guideline

Submit the first three chapters of your completed manuscript to ldpsubmissions@gmail.com, subject line: Your book's title. The manuscript must be in a .doc file and sent as an attachment. Document should be in Times New Roman, double spaced and in size 12 font. Also, provide your synopsis and full contact information. If sending multiple submissions, they must each be in a separate email.

Have a story but no way to send it electronically? You can still submit to LDP/Ca$h Presents. Send in the first three chapters, written or typed, of your completed manuscript to:

LDP: Submissions Dept
Po Box 870494
Mesquite, Tx 75187

DO NOT send original manuscript. Must be a duplicate.

Provide your synopsis and a cover letter containing your full contact information.

Thanks for considering LDP and Ca$h Presents.

BOW DOWN TO MY GANGSTA

By **Ca$h**

TORN BETWEEN TWO

By **Coffee**

THE STREETS STAINED MY SOUL **II**

By **Marcellus Allen**

BLOOD OF A BOSS **VI**

SHADOWS OF THE GAME II

By **Askari**

LOYAL TO THE GAME **IV**

By **T.J. & Jelissa**

A DOPEBOY'S PRAYER **II**

By **Eddie "Wolf" Lee**

IF LOVING YOU IS WRONG… **III**

By **Jelissa**

TRUE SAVAGE **VII**

MIDNIGHT CARTEL II

DOPE BOY MAGIC III

By **Chris Green**

BLAST FOR ME **III**

DUFFLE BAG CARTEL **IV**

A SAVAGE DOPEBOY II

By **Ghost**

A HUSTLER'S DECEIT III

KILL ZONE **II**

Ghost

BAE BELONGS TO ME III

SOUL OF A MONSTER III

By **Aryanna**

THE COST OF LOYALTY **III**

By **Kweli**

CHAINED TO THE STREETS II

By **J-Blunt**

KING OF NEW YORK V

COKE KINGS IV

BORN HEARTLESS IV

By **T.J. Edwards**

GORILLAZ IN THE BAY V

De'Kari

THE STREETS ARE CALLING II

Duquie Wilson

KINGPIN KILLAZ IV

STREET KINGS III

PAID IN BLOOD III

CARTEL KILLAZ IV

Hood Rich

SINS OF A HUSTLA II

ASAD

TRIGGADALE III

Elijah R. Freeman

KINGZ OF THE GAME V

Playa Ray

SLAUGHTER GANG IV

RUTHLESS HEART II

By Willie Slaughter

THE HEART OF A SAVAGE II

By Jibril Williams

FUK SHYT II

By Blakk Diamond

THE DOPEMAN'S BODYGAURD II

By Tranay Adams

TRAP GOD II

By Troublesome

YAYO III

A SHOOTER'S AMBITION II

By S. Allen

GHOST MOB

Stilloan Robinson

KINGPIN DREAMS II

By Paper Boi Rari

CREAM

By Yolanda Moore

SON OF A DOPE FIEND II

By Renta

FOREVER GANGSTA II

By Adrian Dulan

LOYALTY AIN'T PROMISED

By Keith Williams

THE PRICE YOU PAY FOR LOVE II

By Destiny Skai

Ghost

THE LIFE OF A HOOD STAR
By Rashia Wilson
TOE TAGZ II
By Ah'Million
CONFESSIONS OF A GANGSTA II
By Nicholas Lock
PAID IN KARMA II
By **Meesha**
I'M NOTHING WITHOUT HIS LOVE II
By Monet Dragun
CAUGHT UP IN THE LIFE II
By Robert Baptiste

Available Now

RESTRAINING ORDER **I & II**
By **CA$H & Coffee**
LOVE KNOWS NO BOUNDARIES **I II & III**
By **Coffee**
RAISED AS A GOON I, II, III & IV
BRED BY THE SLUMS I, II, III
BLAST FOR ME I & II
ROTTEN TO THE CORE I II III
A BRONX TALE I, II, III
DUFFEL BAG CARTEL I II III
HEARTLESS GOON I II III IV
A SAVAGE DOPEBOY

HEARTLESS GOON I II III

DRUG LORDS I II III

By **Ghost**

LAY IT DOWN **I & II**

LAST OF A DYING BREED

BLOOD STAINS OF A SHOTTA I & II III

By **Jamaica**

LOYAL TO THE GAME

LOYAL TO THE GAME II

LOYAL TO THE GAME III

LIFE OF SIN I, II III

By **TJ & Jelissa**

BLOODY COMMAS I & II

SKI MASK CARTEL I II & III

KING OF NEW YORK I II,III IV

RISE TO POWER I II III

COKE KINGS I II III

BORN HEARTLESS I II III

By **T.J. Edwards**

IF LOVING HIM IS WRONG…I & II

LOVE ME EVEN WHEN IT HURTS I II III

By **Jelissa**

WHEN THE STREETS CLAP BACK I & II III

By **Jibril Williams**

A DISTINGUISHED THUG STOLE MY HEART I II & III

LOVE SHOULDN'T HURT I II III IV

RENEGADE BOYS I II III IV

PAID IN KARMA

By **Meesha**

A GANGSTER'S CODE I &, II III

A GANGSTER'S SYN I II III

THE SAVAGE LIFE I II III

CHAINED TO THE STREETS

By J-Blunt

PUSH IT TO THE LIMIT

By **Bre' Hayes**

BLOOD OF A BOSS **I, II, III, IV, V**

SHADOWS OF THE GAME

By **Askari**

THE STREETS BLEED MURDER **I, II & III**

THE HEART OF A GANGSTA I II& III

By **Jerry Jackson**

CUM FOR ME

CUM FOR ME 2

CUM FOR ME 3

CUM FOR ME 4

CUM FOR ME 5

An **LDP Erotica Collaboration**

BRIDE OF A HUSTLA **I II & II**

THE FETTI GIRLS **I, II& III**

CORRUPTED BY A GANGSTA I, II III, IV

BLINDED BY HIS LOVE

THE PRICE YOU PAY FOR LOVE

By **Destiny Skai**

WHEN A GOOD GIRL GOES BAD
By **Adrienne**
THE COST OF LOYALTY I II
By Kweli
A GANGSTER'S REVENGE **I II III & IV**
THE BOSS MAN'S DAUGHTERS
THE BOSS MAN'S DAUGHTERS II
THE BOSSMAN'S DAUGHTERS III
THE BOSSMAN'S DAUGHTERS IV
THE BOSS MAN'S DAUGHTERS **V**
A SAVAGE LOVE **I & II**
BAE BELONGS TO ME I II
A HUSTLER'S DECEIT I, II, III
WHAT BAD BITCHES DO I, II, III
SOUL OF A MONSTER I II
KILL ZONE
By **Aryanna**
A KINGPIN'S AMBITON
A KINGPIN'S AMBITION **II**
I MURDER FOR THE DOUGH
By **Ambitious**
TRUE SAVAGE
TRUE SAVAGE II
TRUE SAVAGE **III**
TRUE SAVAGE **IV**
TRUE SAVAGE **V**
TRUE SAVAGE **VI**

Ghost

DOPE BOY MAGIC I, II
MIDNIGHT CARTEL
By **Chris Green**
A DOPEBOY'S PRAYER
By **Eddie "Wolf" Lee**
THE KING CARTEL **I, II & III**
By **Frank Gresham**
THESE NIGGAS AIN'T LOYAL **I, II & III**
By **Nikki Tee**
GANGSTA SHYT **I II &III**
By **CATO**
THE ULTIMATE BETRAYAL
By **Phoenix**
BOSS'N UP **I , II & III**
By **Royal Nicole**
I LOVE YOU TO DEATH
By Destiny J
I RIDE FOR MY HITTA
I STILL RIDE FOR MY HITTA
By **Misty Holt**
LOVE & CHASIN' PAPER
By **Qay Crockett**
TO DIE IN VAIN
SINS OF A HUSTLA
By **ASAD**
BROOKLYN HUSTLAZ
By **Boogsy Morina**

BROOKLYN ON LOCK I & II

By **Sonovia**

GANGSTA CITY

By **Teddy Duke**

A DRUG KING AND HIS DIAMOND I & II III

A DOPEMAN'S RICHES

HER MAN, MINE'S TOO I, II

CASH MONEY HO'S

By Nicole Goosby

TRAPHOUSE KING **I II & III**

KINGPIN KILLAZ I II III

STREET KINGS I II

PAID IN BLOOD **I II**

CARTEL KILLAZ I II III

By **Hood Rich**

LIPSTICK KILLAH **I, II, III**

CRIME OF PASSION I II & III

By **Mimi**

STEADY MOBBN' **I, II, III**

THE STREETS STAINED MY SOUL

By **Marcellus Allen**

WHO SHOT YA **I, II, III**

SON OF A DOPE FIEND

Renta

GORILLAZ IN THE BAY **I II III IV**

DE'KARI

TRIGGADALE I II

Ghost

Elijah R. Freeman
GOD BLESS THE TRAPPERS I, II, III
THESE SCANDALOUS STREETS I, II, III
FEAR MY GANGSTA I, II, III
THESE STREETS DON'T LOVE NOBODY I, II
BURY ME A G I, II, III, IV, V
A GANGSTA'S EMPIRE I, II, III, IV
THE DOPEMAN'S BODYGAURD
Tranay Adams
THE STREETS ARE CALLING
Duquie Wilson
MARRIED TO A BOSS... I II III
By Destiny Skai & Chris Green
KINGZ OF THE GAME I II III IV
Playa Ray
SLAUGHTER GANG I II III
RUTHLESS HEART
By Willie Slaughter
THE HEART OF A SAVAGE
By Jibril Williams
FUK SHYT
By Blakk Diamond
DON'T F#CK WITH MY HEART I II
By Linnea
ADDICTED TO THE DRAMA I II III
By Jamila
YAYO I II

A SHOOTER'S AMBITION

By S. Allen

TRAP GOD

By Troublesome

FOREVER GANGSTA

By Adrian Dulan

TOE TAGZ

By Ah'Million

KINGPIN DREAMS

By Paper Boi Rari

CONFESSIONS OF A GANGSTA

By Nicholas Lock

I'M NOTHING WITHOUT HIS LOVE

By Monet Dragun

CAUGHT UP IN THE LIFE

By Robert Baptiste

BOOKS BY LDP'S CEO, CA$H

TRUST IN NO MAN

TRUST IN NO MAN 2

TRUST IN NO MAN 3

BONDED BY BLOOD

SHORTY GOT A THUG

THUGS CRY

THUGS CRY 2

THUGS CRY 3

TRUST NO BITCH

TRUST NO BITCH 2

TRUST NO BITCH 3

TIL MY CASKET DROPS

RESTRAINING ORDER

RESTRAINING ORDER 2

IN LOVE WITH A CONVICT

Coming Soon

BONDED BY BLOOD 2

BOW DOWN TO MY GANGSTA

Heartless Goon 4

www.ingramcontent.com/pod-product-compliance
Lightning Source LLC
Chambersburg PA
CBHW070526260626
47161CB00004B/1640